VEE MORRIS

The Golden Mirror

A forgotten Edinburgh Attic. A golden mirror. A journey through time.

To Clare

A magical encounter in Edinburgh! Its meant to be!

I hope you enjoy reading as much as I enjoyed writing. Vee Morris x

First published by Lantern Gate Press 2025

Copyright © 2025 by Vee Morris

All rights reserved. No part of this publication may be reproduced, stored or transmitted in any form or by any means, electronic, mechanical, photocopying, recording, scanning, or otherwise without written permission from the publisher. It is illegal to copy this book, post it to a website, or distribute it by any other means without permission.

First edition

ISBN: 978-1-9192018-0-1

Early Reader Reviews

Early Reader Reviews

"I would highly recommend this book.... it gripped me straight away with both the characters and location, and extra buzz was if you believe in magic, this is for you. Cannot wait till next book is out to read." **Dawn Lee, Advance Reader.**

"My favourite type of book – one you just can't put down! Complex and intriguing characters are placed in a city that the author obviously loves. Joy in the magic and mystery of life shines through from start to Unish." **LorraineAlexander Clark, Advance Reader.**

"I really liked everything about the book... you get drawn into the whole story, not only the characters, but the history of the places it's set in. I would recommend this book to anyone who likes both history, time travel and mystery. Note to the Author: I'm looking forward to the next chapter in this fascinating adventure." **Olwyn McAloon Peareth, Early Reader.**

"I really enjoyed this book and reading about old Edinburgh. I wonder if Ella will go on more fabulous adventures!" **Paula MᶜFadyen, Early Reader.**

"A beautiful, heart-warming and inspiring story that each day I couldn't wait to read. The author brings the spirit of historic Edinburgh vividly to life with both ordinary and extraordinary magic!"
   Michelle Edinburgh, Advance Reader

Chapter 1

Ella pushed her way through the golden mirror into the attic. She looked around, and the familiar room had transformed, crammed with Victorian trunks, clothes, and toys. A century of time had vanished in a heartbeat.

Ella was a companion to an eccentric elderly lady. Miss Powell was a sharp-eyed, silver-haired woman whose kindness, wisdom, stories and tarot card readings struck a chord with Ella, who believed in all things magical.

Most days, Ella would take a morning walk to blow away the cobwebs. Nearby was a massive, Victorian, derelict asylum that she loved to explore. With its collection of dark, mysterious and yet magical buildings with domes, spires and countless huge windows, it looked like an eccentric castle from a forgotten, dark fairy tale.

Ella never tired of walking around the acres of grounds and buildings; she never tired of imagining its bustling past.

This morning, though, Ella was excited to return to the house. She'd recently ventured up to the dusty, old attic and found a locked door with a beautiful golden mirror on it. When she asked the Miss Powell about it and if she knew where the key might be, Miss Powell said she didn't, but Ella was welcome to look for it and added, 'Be careful not to get lost up there.' *What did she mean by that?* Ella had eventually found a bunch of old keys in the shed.

Back in the house, Ella made her way up the steep, narrow stairs to the attic, her pulse quickening as she held the keys in her hand, hoping one of the keys would fit, and wondered what she might find behind the mirror.

She stepped into the attic and heard Scott, the good-looking handyman she secretly fancied but could never imagine fancying her back. He was hammering on the roof above. The sound was oddly comforting, and Ella liked knowing he was close by.

The floorboards creaked below her feet as she made her way towards the door with the golden mirror. As she got closer, the temperature around her seemed to drop, and it was as if she had stepped into a bubble of cold air. She shivered, pulled her jumper closer to her body and held tight to the keys she had found in the hall cupboard downstairs, hoping that one would unlock the door with the golden mirror.

She was drawn to one particular key from the bunch – a large, gilded key with fancy engraving on it, and it felt heavy and cold. She slid it into the keyhole and turned it anticlockwise. The old workings of the lock clicked and slid, and she was delighted when the key turned.

Ella's pulse raced, and she felt excitement in her stomach. She was sure she was the first person to open this lock in a very long time. She stepped back, glanced at herself in the mirror, and, out of pure habit, ruffled her hair, stuck out her tongue, and smiled at herself.

What would she find behind the golden mirror? Vintage clothes, books, diaries, photographs or – she could barely bring herself to think about it – nothing? She couldn't wait any longer.

She turned the handle, pulled the door open, and looked into the darkness. Behind the mirrored door was a cupboard, but to her disappointment, there was nothing there.

Ella took a deep breath and stepped into the dark space, her hands skimming the cold, rough walls as if she might find something hidden. But there was nothing. The emptiness seemed to mock her, and disappointment surged through her body. She had been so certain – she could almost smell the promise of something exciting lurking behind the locked door.

Even though the cupboard was empty, she was sure she could sense energy in there; she had a sixth sense when she came across what she believed to be a sacred space, and she had that feeling now. She closed the cupboard door and allowed the darkness to envelop her.

CHAPTER 1

She began a simple ritual that she started every sacred moment with. Taking three deep breaths, Ella imagined herself bathed in a pure white light. With each deep breath, she saw in her mind's eye the light at her feet swirling upwards and around her body until she was shrouded in this pure protective light. Now she felt ready to create some magic.

She felt inspired to spin around three times in a clockwise direction, a motion inspired by her love and intrigue with the Rule of Three and Earth Magic.

As she turned for the last time, she took another deep breath, and suddenly she felt herself being whirled around by unseen forces! She held onto the sides of the cupboard to steady herself. She felt as if she had been turned inside out and all the cells in her body had dissipated and were now flying back into place. The air was charged with an energy she hadn't felt before. She steadied herself, took a deep breath, and asked herself - what the hell had just happened?

When she felt able, she opened her eyes. She couldn't quite describe why, but she felt very different and disconnected from her body. She was unsettled and a bit scared and just wanted to step back into the attic, see the familiar surroundings, and hear Scott working on the roof. She was feeling shaken and weird.

She tried to push the door open, but oddly, instead of walking back into the attic, she felt as though she floated through the door and golden mirror. That felt strange, she thought, but she was glad to be out of the cupboard. She took a deep breath, and as she looked around, she couldn't quite believe what she was seeing.

Everything was the same - but different, peculiarly different. The attic was lit up, but the light was much dimmer and more golden. It was completely silent - no sound of Scott hammering on the roof or the sound of traffic outside.

Chapter 2

As she looked in the mirror, a deep scream rose from her stomach into the air because there was no reflection. Nothing. No one. Not a trace or an image of her. And when she screamed, she heard nothing.

What the hell was going on? She was feeling very odd. As she looked around, the attic she knew had changed dramatically. Why couldn't she see her reflection? Why was the attic full of ancient trunks, Victorian clothes, an old-fashioned doll's house and a rocking horse? And why, oh why, couldn't she hear Scott banging on the guttering outside?

She had so many questions and tried to be logical despite what she was seeing around her and the fact that she had no reflection. There was no rational reason for any of it. It was all so surreal.

That's it, she told herself. It must be a dream. I must have fallen asleep in the attic, and now I'm dreaming.

She convinced herself that that was what had happened. It was the only explanation that made sense. She allowed herself to relax a bit. Stop trying to explain everything, and try to enjoy the experience, she told herself.

After a few moments of exploring the attic, she was keen to see what was downstairs. She floated down and seeped through the door into the hall.

She looked around herself. She was still in Miss Powell's house, but it looked as if it was a hundred years ago. It felt dark, old-fashioned, and a bit spooky. She floated into what she knew would be the sitting room, and when she pushed herself through the door, she was happy to see the four enormous bay windows she was familiar with and so fond of looking out of. Taking a closer look around the room, she quickly realised that everything else was

CHAPTER 2

different in here too.

There was a very thick and fancy rug on the floor instead of a fitted carpet. The fireplace was the same but had a vast, heavy-framed mirror above it. Somebody had filled the fire grate with hot coals and warmed the room nicely. There were two high-backed chairs, a fine-looking writing desk, a chaise lounge, and bookshelves filled with many interesting old books. The windows were framed with heavy, dark burgundy curtains. It was all very different from the living room Ella was familiar with.

She floated over to the windows, but instead of looking out onto the immense oak trees at the bottom of the garden, Ella could see straight over to the Pentland Hills. There were some trees at the bottom of the garden, but they were young and small.

When she wasn't dreaming, the house that she lived in had a large patio with steps down to the grass. However, in this version of the house, the garden in her dream had a large vegetable patch full of healthy-looking plants. She could see fruit trees and a glasshouse where the garage usually was. The garden looked beautifully manicured and well-maintained.

Satisfied that she had seen everything in this room, she floated out of the sitting room. She was intrigued to see the rest of the house. To the right of the hall was the kitchen. It was the same shape as the kitchen in her world, but again, very different. No fridge freezer or gas hob to be seen. Instead, there was an enormous Aga stove, with big pots on it, bubbling away. She looked around the kitchen, taking it all in.

Against the wall was a large Welsh dresser full of beautiful hand-painted plates and bowls. The shelves all around the walls were full of square tins, jars, bottles and small sacks full of flour and grains. There were other jars of dried fruits, beans, and things she did not recognise.

There were some dishes in a vast Belfast sink, but everything else was sparkly clean. Everything felt so real and vivid.

Ella heard a bell and looked in the direction from which she had heard the noise. She looked up and saw a large board with seven fancy bells on it, and underneath each bell was the name of a room - drawing room, master bedroom, bedroom 2, bedroom 3, dining room, drawing room 2, conservatory.

It was the bell in bedroom two that was moving and ringing. 'Blimey,' thought Ella, 'this house isn't so big that it needs bells!' She giggled to herself. Even in her dreams, she was ever practical.

She continued to float through the house, taking in the furniture, heavy drapes, and oversized fancy rugs, revealing polished wooden floors underneath.

In each room, there was what looked like a doorbell on the wall, usually next to the fireplace, and she suspected they rang the bells in the kitchen for servants to hear. She heard the service bell ring again.

A young woman appeared in the hall, wearing a black dress down to her calves, a white apron, a white lace cap, and carrying a feather duster. To Ella, she looked like a maid from times gone by.

She was just about to ask her a question when she felt the maid walk right through her. It was the strangest sensation. Ella felt her energy and cells dissipate through the air and then experienced them coming back together again, so she was whole - well, as whole as an invisible entity, which she was at this moment, could be!

What a strange feeling, she thought. But it confirmed that in this dream, she couldn't be seen. Ella wasn't sure what was happening. This was not usually how her dreams felt. But, if this wasn't a dream, where was she and what had happened to her?

The maid scurried to the other side of the house and went into what was Ella's room in her world.

Ella was curious and decided to follow. She floated through the door and into a beautiful bedroom. Again, she had the sensation of familiarity. The room was the same shape as her bedroom, and the four bay windows were the same, but that was where the similarity ended. She felt like she was stepping into a stately home. It was furnished so grandly.

There was a large rug on the wooden floor, a lovely fireplace with a fire crackling away, giving the room a gorgeous, warm glow, and a large silver-framed mirror hung above it. There was a huge wooden double bed, beautifully made up with silk pillows and throws.

CHAPTER 2

There was an elegant dressing table with a vase of beautiful fresh-cut flowers and an array of beautiful crystal bottles of all shapes and sizes, jars, and brushes. Against the wall was a large, opulent wardrobe with a long mirror, and beside this, an upright, blue, cushioned chair positioned to look out the window.

Standing at the window, with her back to the room, stood a tall, slim woman with dark hair cut into a short bob. Her long, green dress fell to her calves, dropped at the waist and showed off her fine figure.

The woman turned around when she heard the door open, and Ella got her next fright of the day. The woman looked almost exactly like her!

Chapter 3

This experience was getting stranger and stranger. Ella looked at the woman in front of her, and without a doubt, she looked very similar to her reflection - the same, but different. The woman in front of her had a different hairstyle, clothes and makeup, but her bone structure, posture and body type were almost identical to Ella's. She looked at the woman in front of her again and admired her. She looked stunning - similar to Ella, but yet brighter and sharper and confident.

Ella was shaken out of her thoughts by the maid.

'Morning, ma'am, you rang the bell,' she said.

'Yes,' said the woman, 'I'm looking for the outfit I wear when volunteering at the asylum - do you know where it is?' Her voice even sounded like Ella's but with a softer tone and a slightly broader Scottish accent.

'It's still drying, ma'am,' said the maid. 'I'll check it right away,' and she turned to leave.

'That's fine, Alison, as long as it's dry for later in the week. And Alison?'

'Yes ma'am?'

'I've asked you many times, please call me Lily, not ma'am. You make me sound so old, and it sounds so formal.'

'If the master heard me call you Lily, I'd get a clip round the ear,' said Alison. 'Also, it doesn't feel right.' And with that, the maid bustled away.

Ella was intrigued by the house and its characters. It all felt so real. She found herself not wanting to leave Lily and stayed in the room.

Lily pottered around the bedroom, stood in front of the mirror fixing her hair, put on some bold, darkish brown lipstick, and gave herself a spray of

CHAPTER 3

perfume from one of the many beautiful crystal spray bottles on her dressing table. Ella could smell the light fragrance. Wait a minute, Ella thought. A dream that I can hear and smell? Now that is unusual.

Much as Ella was enjoying the situation, whilst she told herself it was a dream, things were getting stranger by the minute. She tried telling herself to wake up, but nothing around her changed.

Ella knew that even in her wildest and most vivid of dreams, she could not smell, hear or feel that she was a floating ball of energy.

She wondered if she was astral projecting. As a child, she'd sometimes leave her body in sleep and float high above the world below.

She wondered, am I astral projecting now? But she didn't think so. This experience felt very different. She knew that this strange sensation had something to do with the golden mirror in the attic. Ever since she'd stepped back out of the mirror, things had felt very weird.

She could not help but think it looked as it would have looked a hundred years ago, and began to feel more than a little scared.

'What if I am in some weird vortex of time and I can't get back to my own time?' Ella felt panic rising from her stomach. She whirled around, taking in the surrounding scene, and tried to think logically about the situation.

There was no logic. Ella knew she was in the same house where she currently lived, but this was a different time. She knew she wasn't dreaming. She began to believe that somehow, she had travelled back in time. Frightened though she was, it also fascinated her to be in a different era.

Ella was brought back to the moment when Lily, walking to the other side of the room, unknowingly walked right through Ella.

As the woman passed through her, Ella felt her energy stick to the lady and now felt attached and almost felt part of her. When the woman moved, she moved; when she touched her hair, Ella felt her hair; and when she moved her legs, Ella felt it too.

Ella had somehow been absorbed into the woman's body. Lily stepped out of the room, into the hall and opened up the lobby door. There was a selection of coats, hats, gloves, scarves, boots and shoes in there. She called out, to no one in particular, it seemed, 'Just going out for a wee walk.'

Lily pulled on a coat, hat and gloves, opened the door and stepped outside. Ella felt part of her – feeling every movement as if it were her own.

Chapter 4

Lily stepped out into the fresh but chilly day, and Ella could even feel the cold, crisp air on her skin. She was slightly creeped out by being absorbed into someone else's body - even if the body did look a bit like her.

At this moment, it did not feel as if she had a choice in where her energy was placed. She wondered what kind of magic had brought her to this moment.

It was like an *Alice in Wonderland* experience or some magic mushroom trip.

Ella had experimented with magic mushrooms when she was younger, experiencing some profound and sometimes challenging hallucinogenic moments. While her friends took them for fun, Ella used them as a tool for self-discovery. She had the most incredible journeys and immersed herself in books on ancient spiritual and shamanic practices, learning about the use of mind-altering plants such as mushrooms.

She loved the feeling of being part of another world. On many journeys, she met spirit guides, animals, and fairies. She loved that they shared their world with her.

However, she'd had a couple of bad trips that left her anxious and scared. In those moments, she focused on her breathing, slowing her heartbeat until the fear faded.

She wanted to believe this was just a magic mushroom flashback, not an actual trip back in time. But deep down, she knew otherwise.

She took deep breaths, calming herself, and decided to go with the flow for now, even if it felt strange. Being attached to this woman was odd.

Lily stepped out into the well-manicured garden with its perfect hedges, spring flowers, and lush lawn. *Someone works hard here,* Ella thought.

Now calmer, she took in the surroundings. The only houses nearby were the four that Miss Powell's belonged to. In her world, there were rows of semi-detached and terraced houses. Here, there was space and countryside. The hill in front of the house was topped by a well-trodden dirt track instead of a concrete road.

Lily walked up the hill. Around the corner came a cart pulled by a beautiful Clydesdale horse.

'Morning, ma'am,' said the older man, tipping his hat. Beside him sat a handsome young man covered in coal dust, who gave Lily a cheeky grin. The cart was full of loose bags of coal.

'Morning,' said Lily. 'It's a bright and beautiful day.'

'Aye, that it is, ma'am.' The cart trundled down the hill.

Even though Ella didn't understand what was happening, she wanted to explore this world on her own. Lily was walking too slowly, so Ella focused on detaching herself from her host body. She felt the cold air around her as she floated free, watching Lily from a distance.

She recognised a couple of houses that normally would have been surrounded by others. Here, they stood alone.

Lily was heading towards Craighouse, the old asylum grounds - one of Ella's favourite places to walk. They floated through the archway into the hospital grounds. The copse of trees ahead was younger, full of skinny saplings instead of the established woodland she knew. A dirt track cut through the grass, with benches along the way.

The asylum building took her breath away. With its grand red and brown stone turrets, and countless windows. Villas surrounded the main building, interconnected in Victorian splendour.

On the grass hill in front of the asylum were people in 1920s-style clothes. Nurses in white starched uniforms and peaked caps walked and chatted. Tennis courts, a bowling green, a vegetable garden, pigs, sheep, and outbuildings made the place look like a working smallholding.

An elderly man, accompanied by a nurse, strolled past. 'Morning, ma'am.' Lily returned the greeting.

The penny dropped. The people in plain clothes were patients, and those in uniform were staff. Somehow, she was seeing the asylum in full use as if she had stepped back in time.

Her anxiety gone, Ella felt free and elated, eager to explore. But Lily had other ideas and headed back towards the house.

Ella lingered for one last look before floating after her.

Chapter 5

Lily walked slowly back to her house, opened the front door, and stepped into the lobby. She removed her hat, gloves, and boots, then went into her bedroom and lay down. She appeared to fall asleep quickly.

Ella was unsettled. She just wanted to wake up or do whatever it took to return to her familiar bedroom.

She floated through the bedroom door into the old-fashioned hall. She imagined herself back in Miss Powell's house, surrounded by familiar things. But when she opened her eyes, she was still in the same old-fashioned house.

Her heart sped up, breath shortening, anxiety rising from her stomach to her throat. She took deep breaths.

That made her giggle. If this were a weird mushroom flashback, logic wouldn't exist.

Giggling helped. Endorphins flowed, and she relaxed.

Perhaps this was like a shamanic journey - and in those, you returned to where you began to find your way home.

She floated back up to the attic. The beautiful, familiar, golden mirrored door was waiting. She pushed her energy through it into the dark space behind.

Okay, she told herself, *I'm ready to go back now.*

She opened her eyes and pushed her energy back into the attic, but to her dismay, it was still filled with Victorian toys, trunks, and photographs.

She began to panic. What had she done differently the first time?

Then she remembered. She had turned clockwise three times.

She pushed through the mirror again, took a deep breath, visualised Miss

CHAPTER 5

Powell's attic, and spun three times the other way, repeating, *I want to return* – a bit like Dorothy in *The Wizard of Oz*.

The world spun. She held the cupboard sides to keep her balance.

Whoa, that was trippy, she thought, touching the solid handle of the mirror door. She stepped out into the attic.

Relief flooded her. She was back among her own suitcases and boxes, and she could hear Scott hammering on the roof.

She turned to the mirror and smiled at her reflection. She'd never been so glad to see herself.

Chapter 6

Ella was confused. What the hell had just happened?

The attic looked exactly as it had earlier that day. She made her way downstairs into the hall, feeling the familiar carpet under her feet.

In the kitchen, she put the kettle on, then stepped outside. A huge lavender bush grew against the fence by the neighbour's house. She squeezed a flower, inhaling its comforting scent.

She checked that the garden was just a lawn with flower borders - no vegetable plot. Good.

She could remember every detail of the old house, Alison the maid, Lily, the neighbourhood, and the asylum. Closing her eyes, she could still see them as if they stood before her.

She sat in her favourite garden chair, reclined slightly, and closed her eyes to think.

'Alright for some,' Scott said, stepping into the garden.

Ella sat up.

Scott, Miss Powell's handyman, worked at the house most weeks - a definite bonus in her opinion. Fit, good-looking, and with a great smile, he was the focus of her wee crush. It made her self-conscious and tongue-tied around him, convinced he was out of her league.

'Aye, well,' she said. 'It's been a long and weird day so far.'

'Long day? It's not even lunchtime,' Scott laughed. *That's odd,* she thought. *It felt like I was away for hours.* 'I've still got a bit of work to do, but maybe...' Scott hesitated. 'Maybe we could have a cup of tea later?'

Scott's gaze lingered, and Ella caught what might have been a hint of

CHAPTER 6

attraction in Scott's eyes – or was she imagining it?

But she was too distracted, still replaying the morning's events. Without thinking, she dismissed him.

'I don't think so. I've got to clear my head.' She glanced up and caught what might have been disappointment in his eyes.

As he walked away, she wondered if she'd made a mistake. Maybe he liked her more than she thought. She almost called after him but stopped herself. *I probably just imagined it,* she thought.

Chapter 7

Ella returned to the house, made herself a cup of tea, and retreated to her bedroom. Curling up on the sofa, she looked around. It was strange remembering how it looked a hundred years ago.

She thought back to what she'd seen through the golden mirror - the Aga oven, the kitchen, the old-fashioned furniture, rugs, and the way Lily and the maid were dressed. Their calf-length dresses draped at the hips, and Lily's sharp bob screamed 1920s. Yes, it had to be a hundred years ago.

She recalled the walk up to the asylum and seeing it at the peak of its use. When it was fully operational, there would have been hundreds of staff to keep it going, not to mention the number of patients.

The more Ella thought about it, the more it felt like she'd somehow travelled back in time to life in the house and asylum a hundred years ago - or more.

She brought herself back to the present moment. Wait a minute, did Scott ask her to have a chat and a cup of tea later? Did she dismiss him and say no? What was she thinking? Yesterday, she would have knocked him down in her enthusiasm to agree.

But it wasn't yesterday. It was today, and something strange had happened, and Ella was determined to figure out what and why she suddenly had such a clear vision of what this house and the surrounding area looked like a hundred years ago. For the rest of the day, Ella pottered about the house, lost in a daydream.

The next morning, as she woke up slowly, her first thought was of the golden mirror in the attic and the strange experience she'd had yesterday. She put her foot gingerly onto the bedroom floor. 'Damn, it's cold!' She said.

CHAPTER 7

Springtime in Scotland was a beautiful time of year. This morning, though, it still felt like winter. She might try to persuade Miss Powell to reset the heating so it came on earlier in the morning again.

Ella was very fond of Miss Powell; she was an interesting woman - that was for sure. She was forever drinking herbal teas and taking her tinctures from tiny bottles. Ella wondered where she had obtained all her herb teas and tinctures. They were never on any shopping list she gave to Ella.

Miss Powell liked to potter about in the herb section in her back garden, then disappear into the front room for a few hours. Maybe that's where she kept her selection of herbs, thought Ella.

It was the only room in the house that Ella had never been into. Every time she walked past it, a lovely combination of scents emanated from it. She must ask her about it one day, but so far, Miss Powell had made no invitation to her to look in the room, and Ella was okay with that.

Ella and Miss Powell enjoyed each other's company, and she enjoyed working for her. The job was live-in, in a big, old house in the South of Edinburgh, and not so far from the city centre whenever she wanted to venture in.

It suited her on many levels. There was no rent to pay, and the house had many rooms, so she had plenty of space. She loved her bedroom, with its four bay windows, double bed and comfy sofa. There was a lovely garden - tended by Scott - that she could potter in when the mood took her.

She had two days off a week and every evening to herself, and her work was easygoing.

Miss Powell enjoyed having Ella around to help with household chores, cook her meals, and be a companion. The house was old-fashioned and dusty, but very comfortable. Ella kept on top of it as best she could, and Miss Powell seemed happy with her service.

The job also suited her because, if she was honest, she didn't quite know what else she would be doing with her life.

She was twenty-eight, as her sister Janey kept on reminding her. The two sisters could not be any more different, but they only had each other and their adopted mum, and Ella tried to keep as close as she could - given Janey's comparatively chaotic lifestyle.

However, not having to think about her career, travel, and future suited her just fine at the moment. Okay, her job and, let's face it, her life could be a little predictable sometimes, but Ella escaped by consuming novels, spiritual and self-help books by the dozen! She told herself this was okay for now, and she was happy and content with her lot.

Ella got up and threw on some clothes, not caring too much about what she wore as long as it was comfortable. She put her long, dark hair into a clasp and pulled it up into a messy bun. She went through her morning ritual of washing her face, applying her homemade skin cream, and brushing her teeth in the small sink in her room. As she looked in the mirror, she scrunched up her face, stuck her tongue out and laughed at herself.

She stepped out of her large bedroom into the soft, deep carpeted hall, and padded her way along to the kitchen. As expected, there was a saucepan on the stove with porridge made with water and salt left out for her. Miss Powell would have been up for hours already, and always left some porridge out for her, and Ella was used to her ways. She ate her porridge whilst waiting for the kettle to boil to make a cup of tea for them both.

Chapter 8

As Ella made the tea, she thought about what she would do that day. It was her day off. She might venture back up into the attic again and try to find more about it.

Ella set up the tea tray for her and Miss Powell, picked it up and made her way to the front of the house. She pushed the door open with her shoulder and stepped into the lovely, bright sitting room.

This room was one of her favourites in the house. It had four enormous windows overlooking the garden and onto the big, old trees beyond. It was south-facing, so even on the greyest of days, the room filled with light.

Miss Powell was sitting in her rocking chair with the morning paper. 'Morning, Ella,' she said and went back to her paper.

'Morning,' Ella said, put the tray down on the stool and poured their tea.

'You know, you don't have to bring tea in on your day off.'

'It's no bother,' said Ella, 'I enjoy my cuppa tea in the morning with you, though, and it's always lovely to get the low down and gossip of the day from the paper.'

Miss Powell quietly chuckled behind her newspaper. 'Not much to report today, but I'll keep you posted,' she said.

Ella's eyes wandered over to the purple silk cloth on the table next to Miss Powell. She knew that within the silk cloth were the most beautiful, ancient tarot cards.

Ella loved it when Miss Powell unwrapped her cards and asked her if she had a question. Whenever Miss Powell gave her a tarot reading, the cards gave her some clarity on whatever subject she was focusing on.

Miss Powell had the beautiful gift of being able to read the cards and relate to Ella what she already knew deep down, but needed to hear from another source. She couldn't explain the magic of the cards; she just knew they spoke to her.

Ella curled up on the big, comfy sofa, looking out the window and admiring one of her favourite birds, a robin, sitting on a branch of the blossom tree in the garden. The wind was swaying the trees in the background, and it was a peaceful, sunny day. Her mind wandered to the attic and what had happened when she went behind the golden mirror the day before.

Casually, Ella remarked, 'I was up in the attic yesterday and wondered about the door with the golden mirror on it.'

Miss Powell put down her newspaper and said, 'To be honest, lass, I've not had a reason to go up there for a long time.'

Ella wasn't sure if she was ready to share her strange experience of the golden mirror yet. 'I found the key and just wondered if you knew anything about it?'

'I'm sure I've heard stories of that golden mirror,' said Miss Powell, 'but for the life of me I can't remember them right now,' and went back to her paper and cup of tea.

I wish she could remember, thought Ella, but she hasn't said no about going up there. She felt that she had got the thumbs up for exploring the attic, and looked forward to going back up again later.

Ella was a daydreamer and always created stories. She could see magic in the most everyday things that other people thought were boring. Already in her mind's eye, she could see herself exploring the attic again and discovering what might lie behind the door with the golden mirror. She finished her cup of tea, gathered up the tray, took it into the kitchen, cleaned up, and then she was ready for the day ahead.

Ella often started her day off with a walk that allowed her to shake off the cobwebs and enjoy the beauty of the day. She got ready and was eager to go out, keen to see what adventures awaited her.

Chapter 9

Ella stepped out, looking forward to her five-minute walk to the old asylum and forest. She pulled her coat close around her. The crisp, early spring day hinted at the beauty yet to come. She loved this time of year.

As she walked through the huge gates and turned into the grounds, she looked over at the old asylum. Ella was fascinated by the building and would often wander around the old, disused buildings. After yesterday's experience of what felt like travelling back in time, Ella could now see in her mind's eye what the hospital actually looked like when it was up and running.

This morning, she felt the need to be in the woods and walked into them. She took in deep gulps of fresh, crisp air and walked through the forest, feeling much better just for being out in the open air. There was an avenue of enormous oak trees, leading to a forest of pine, chestnut and other old trees. This morning, there were big puddles to jump over, and when she got to the edge of the forest, she felt like she was on the edge of the world.

From here, she could see the whole of Edinburgh in all her glory, from Arthur's Seat to the castle, across to the Firth of Forth estuary. On a clear day, she could see for miles and would sit there, getting lost in the view.

She sighed at the beauty of it all. She found sitting in nature so healing. After a while, she began to make her way back through the forest, into the grounds and through the stone archway back onto the street.

As she made her way down the hill, she could see Miss Powell's house on the corner. As she got closer, she could see a beat-up old work van with S J Handyman written on the side.

Ah, she thought, *Scott is working around the house today.* Knowing he would be around made her smile; his presence always brightened her day. She enjoyed the casual banter between them and had to admit that she fancied him a bit. He was fit, good-looking, and seemed like a genuinely lovely guy as well. She couldn't believe she turned down the chance to sit down with him yesterday. She could kick herself for being so silly and thoughtless. *That's what happens when I daydream too much,* she thought.

Ella knew a little about Scott from Miss Powell. He was from the other side of the city. He grew up on one of the large housing estates that became famous thanks to Trainspotting, a film made in the 90's about Edinburgh. He was a bit of a rough diamond in some ways, but his heart was in the right place. He had been doing odd jobs for Miss Powell for years, well before Ella took up her work there.

Scott would always quote Miss Powell very reasonably for any jobs she needed to be done, and also came in once or twice a week to keep on top of the garden. He and Miss Powell had a great mutual respect.

As she approached the house, sure enough, there was Scott, up a ladder, checking the guttering. He was wearing work shorts, Dr Marten boots, and a white T-shirt. Ella slowed down a bit to admire his strong calves, nice butt and muscular back and arms. His blond hair glinted in the early spring sunlight, and she had to admit - he was looking good.

She opened the gate, and it clanged shut behind her. It was loud enough for Scott to hear. He turned his head, saw Ella and gave her a cheeky grin. His ice-blue eyes pierced into hers. She gave him a nod and a half-smile, and she let herself into the house.

Ella had no idea how Scott felt about her. As far as she was concerned, he smiled at her and was polite, but she felt that was more because they both worked for Miss Powell. *Let's face it,* Ella thought, *a guy as good-looking as him is not going to be interested in me.*

Ella had no idea that every time Scott saw Ella, his mouth went dry and his stomach tumbled. In his eyes, she was gorgeous. The way she walked with her head high, tossing her long, dark hair, seemed as though she didn't have a care in the world. When she smiled, her sea-blue eyes crinkled and her whole face lit up.

CHAPTER 9

Ella was convinced that she was not the usual type of girl that he would fancy, and that his girlfriends were usually petite, blonde, and high-maintenance.

Ella was the opposite. She was slim but curvy, tall with dark hair, and never seemed overly worried about how she looked; she always looked great to him.

Scott was used to women falling for him without him having to do much. Sometimes he didn't even notice when the women were hitting on him. So, it was a bit of a mystery, and if he was honest, it hurt his pride a bit that Ella seemed to be more aloof and turned him down yesterday.

He turned back to the job he was doing, unsure what reaction to expect after yesterday's rebuff.

Chapter 10

Miss Powell was in her sitting room, Scott was working outside, and Ella had the rest of the day ahead of her. She was thinking about the attic and the bizarre experience she'd had. She was unsure what to do next, but couldn't stop thinking that something very unique had happened yesterday.

She knew she had to go behind the golden mirror again. She went into the hall and opened the little door that led to the steep stairs to the attic, closed the door behind her and made her way up the stairs. The little door at the top of the stairs creaked loudly through lack of use, and just to the left of the wall, there was an old-fashioned light switch. She switched it on and the naked, single light bulb came on.

Did she miss something yesterday? Anything that might explain what had happened? There were old trunks and boxes, a few cobwebs, and piles of papers, along with photo albums and clothes scattered around. Everything intrigued her, but nothing seemed particularly unusual or out of place. The only way was to step behind the golden mirror again and find out once and for all if she could return to that dream-like state, or if it was just her imagination playing tricks on her.

She picked up the bunch of keys, but couldn't remember which key was the one that turned the lock. Once or twice, it almost felt like she'd got the right one, but it didn't slide and click into place. Now there was only one key left to try.

Just then, in the distance, she heard the doorbell chime. Damn, she thought. She waited, wondering if Miss Powell or Scott would get it. Nope, there it goes again.

CHAPTER 10

Ella sighed. She looked around her, wondering where to hide the keys. She slipped them out of sight under the carpet and made her way downstairs. She opened the front door, and there stood her sister Janey.

'Hiya,' said Janey, 'I tried calling you, but no answer as usual! What's the point of having a mobile if you don't carry it around, eh?' She pushed past Ella and made her way into her sister's bedroom.

Janey was smaller than Ella, her lengthy hair glinting with blonde highlights, cascading over her shoulders as if she'd just walked out of a shampoo advert.

She had high cheekbones, full lips, sparkly green eyes and a smattering of freckles over her button nose. Janey was much more into clothes and fashion than Ella ever was. Today, she was wearing flared jeans with high boots peeking out from underneath, a little vest top and a denim jacket. The flared jeans hugged her backside, showcasing her curves and shapely legs, while her green necklace accentuated the green in her eyes. As always, she looked stunning.

Ella followed her in as Janey slumped down on her old comfy sofa, grabbed Ella's bottle of water and slugged it down.

'See that Scott, your handyman, is around,' she said. 'He's looking good in his tight shorts.' She giggled at the thought.

'He is not my handyman, Janey, but yes, I guess he is looking good,' Ella admitted.

'Seriously, Ella, you need to get out of this dusty house more and live a little. You can't spend the rest of your days cooped up here looking after the old woman. A little bit of fun with the local handyman could be just what you need.'

Ella sighed. 'I keep telling you. I'm quite happy doing what I am doing,' she said indignantly. 'I like looking after Miss Powell and this house. It gives me the time to do what I want to do, and to be honest, I'm quite happy being single right now.'

Ella didn't want to tell Janey that she did fancy Scott, but didn't feel confident on any level that he would like her back in the same way. Ella had a terrible habit of thinking and saying negative things about herself. Her self-confidence was not great, hence her collection of self-help books. Maybe one day I'll pluck up the courage to tell him how I feel, she thought to herself. But that thought was best left unsaid to Janey.

Ella was sure that Scott had only asked to hang out with her at lunchtime as he had nothing else to do. He couldn't possibly like or fancy her, could he? She thought of herself as someone that he might want to hang out with out of boredom, but nothing more.

Completely unaware of how Ella was feeling, Janey carried on. 'What you need to be doing, girl, is putting yourself out there a bit. Perhaps a bit of internet dating, or would you like me to ask your handyman out on a date with you? I've seen the way he looks at you.'

'The way he looks at me?' Ella said in surprise, 'I know you think you can read men really well, Janey, but I hate to tell you - you are so off the scale with this one.' Ella's cheeks went red just thinking about it. 'So, please don't!' She said, alarmed at the very thought of the embarrassment of him saying no and even putting him in that position in the first place. 'Don't you dare! He probably has a little blonde thing running around after him when he gets home. Anyway, he wouldn't look twice at me.'

'I wouldn't be so sure,' said Janey, 'but it's your loss.'

As expected, Janey soon moved on to a subject she was much more interested in - herself. 'I'm meeting up with the usual crew tonight at The Waverley Pub, you know the one, just off the High Street. I was calling you to get you to come down. You should come and have some fun with us - a few drinks, a laugh and maybe a pizza later.' Janey stopped to take a breath. Ella could see that Janey was looking forward to the night. 'We'll be there at about seven,' with the total presumption that her sister would do what she expected.

'Thanks,' Ella said, 'I'll think about it.' She hesitated, thinking about her sister's boyfriend. 'Is Rab going to be there?'

'No chance,' said Janey, 'he's working the night shift, so he doesn't even need to know that I'm going out.'

'I don't get it, Janey. Why do you want to be with a guy whom you can't even tell you are going out for a night with your mates? He's so possessive. I

CHAPTER 10

don't understand your obsession with him.'

'He's all right,' said Janey, getting all defensive, 'he just likes to know what I'm up to when he's working. It's obvious - it's because he loves me so much. Anyway, stop trying to pick holes in my relationship - it's your life that's boring and needs help. I'm fine!'

Ella wondered why Janey felt the need to be so defensive. Something didn't feel right. She worried about what lengths this guy, Rab, would go to in order to try to control Janey.

'Have you seen Mum recently?' asked Janey, clearly not quite wanting to go just yet, but wanting to change the subject. 'She keeps calling, asking if I'm all right - have you been saying anything to her?'

Ella shook her head. 'No, she just likes to know what's going on in our lives.' The sisters exchanged glances. 'I know she's not our real mum, but she has been great to us, Janey.'

'Aye, I suppose so. I met a few people who were split up when they were placed into foster care. I guess we were lucky to get to stay together after the accident.'

The sisters still found it hard to talk about the day their mum and dad went out for their anniversary dinner, and never came back. A lorry went into the side of their car and they both died instantly. The sisters were young when it happened, and their lives changed immediately. They knew they were lucky to only live in a few foster homes before their adoptive mum and dad took them in for good. They did love their adopted mum, but bloodwise, they only had each other. For this reason, the sisters kept close, despite their differences and the occasional difficulties in their relationship.

'I'll give Mum a call soon,' said Janey, never one for talking too much about her emotions. Ella knew the subject was closed for now. She picked up her bag and got up to go. 'I'll see you tonight,' and just like that, she was gone.

Before she left the house, Janey knocked on the sitting room door and popped in to say hello and goodbye to Miss Powell. They'd been raised with manners, and she always liked to make a good impression wherever she went.

She knew that Miss Powell liked to see who was coming and going in her house, and a young, fresh face always made her smile. Janey asked her how she was, how her garden was coming along, listened politely and then said her goodbyes.

As she walked up the garden path, she turned and shouted up to Scott, 'Nice legs!' and gave him a cheeky wink and a grin, and then she was off.

Janey had a history of wildness and bad choices of partners over the years. She gave the impression to all that everything was fabulous in her world. She would turn up like a whirlwind, spin everyone around who was in the vicinity and then disappear off to her next venture.

Ella moved over to the sofa where Janey had been sitting, and the space was still warm. She curled up like a cat, licking the wounds that her sister had brought out into the open.

She could hear Scott chopping up wood outside, the birds in the trees, the traffic passing by and the bus trundling up the hill. All the familiar sounds of her life.

Perhaps, she thought, she did need to do something a bit different. She hugged the knowledge to herself that she may have found a magical portal to another world through the golden mirror. To her, that was exciting and stepping into the unknown – but would she ever experience that again?

Chapter 11

Janey's visit had left Ella feeling a bit drained and vulnerable. The excitement of going up to the golden mirror had faded, and Ella decided she wasn't in the best mood to explore the attic that day after all. She needed to ground herself and take some time outdoors.

She loved feeling the earth between her fingers and breathing in the scent of the plants. It helped her clear her head, and she found it healing and therapeutic.

Connecting with the earth, the trees and the plants was important to her. She particularly loved the part of the garden dedicated to growing herbs, and she was becoming more familiar with the plants every day, appreciating their distinctive looks and smells.

She came across a small plant that she didn't recognise and looked around for Scott. If he were close by, she would ask him what it was. He was good at recognising and naming the plants and flowers in the garden, but he was nowhere to be seen.

She walked round to the front of the house and saw that his van was gone. Her heart sank a little when she saw that his van was not there. She'd taken it for granted that he would be around all day, and she was disappointed that he'd gone. She could have kicked herself for not going for lunch with him. Chances like that didn't come along every day, and it's unlikely she'll get another invitation anytime soon, thanks to her not appearing to be interested in spending time with him.

Had she missed her chance because she was so busy daydreaming about – what exactly was she daydreaming about?

Ella was often told she was a daydreamer – more often by her sister than anyone else. That reminded her – she was meant to be going to the pub with Janey tonight.

At that moment, she didn't feel like going. The thought of sitting inside a pub with friends of Janey's as they got more drunk and boisterous didn't appeal that much.

She was sure that if she didn't turn up, Janey would hardly notice. She lingered by the garden gate, picturing the noisy pub, the half-drunk laughter, and Janey's friends talking over each other. The thought made her shoulders tighten. No, not tonight, she decided, returning to the house and into the sitting room. Miss Powell was reading a book and listening to some classical music on her old radio.

She looked up as Ella came into the room. 'I thought Janey said you were meeting up tonight?' Miss Powell asked.

'I was going to go, but don't think I'll bother,' said Ella. She was more interested in finding out more about the house. 'I was up in the attic yesterday, and it made me wonder about the history of this house. It is an interesting old house.'

'Aye, it is that lass. I was very fortunate to grow up here,' said Miss Powell, putting down her book, always happy to talk. 'I've lived here since I was a young girl. My family moved here, oh, way back in the 1940s, I think.'

Miss Powell realised she hadn't talked much about her life in this house, either with Ella or anyone else, for a very long time.

She remembered when the house bustled with visitors, all eager to spend time with her mother, and later with her. But those years were all forgotten, and most of the people had moved out of the neighbourhood a long time ago.

'Do you know how old it is?' asked Ella.

'Well, let me think. Probably, well over one hundred and fifty years at least, I think.' Miss Powell stared off into the distance, and Ella could see a wealth of memories flicker over her face. Ella wondered what experiences she had gone through in her life.

She had asked a few times about her life, but Miss Powell seemed reluctant to share many of her own stories. Ella had a sense that there were depths to

CHAPTER 11

Miss Powell that she had yet to discover or learn about.

'I would love to know more about this house and the family who used to live here,' pondered Ella. 'There aren't many left around here that would remember that family. It was such a long time ago,' said Miss Powell.

'Perhaps, you can tell me one day,' said Ella.

'Och, you don't want to be listening to the stories of an old woman,' said Miss Powell, picking up her book again and closing that particular conversation.

Chapter 12

Ella could see Miss Powell's deck of beautiful tarot cards sitting on the table next to her rocking chair. She was beginning to believe that Miss Powell came from a long line of readers, gypsies and healers and wondered how she'd ended up in this house.

She had been intrigued by tarot cards ever since she was a young teenager and had a few packs of her own.

She felt that today would be a good day for reading, and so asked, 'I feel like I could do with a bit of guidance today. Can you pull a tarot card for me?'

'Of course.' She put down her book, picked up her cards and unwrapped them from the beautiful purple silk bag, then held them close to her heart, closed her eyes and said, 'Ooh, I can feel their energy today. I feel they have something to tell you for sure.'

They were incredible cards and Ella loved them. Every single one was beautifully hand-painted and very old. They had gold leaf painted around the edges, and each card was beautifully illustrated.

Miss Powell had once told Ella about how she had been gifted the cards from her mother, more than 60 years ago, and even then, they were old and beautiful-a bit like Miss Powell herself.

The designs on the cards reminded Ella of Italian Renaissance paintings – soft colours, flowing robes, and eyes that seemed to follow you. Gold leaf edged each card, catching the light as Miss Powell shuffled.

Ella knew enough about tarot to recognise the difference between the Major Arcana and the rest. The twenty-two Major cards told the big life stories – The Magician, The Hermit, Strength – each one carrying a lesson or turning

CHAPTER 12

point. The rest of the deck was made up of suits: Wands, Cups, Pentacles, and Swords, each with its own everyday themes.

She had her own interpretations for the cards, learned from books and the many readings she'd done herself, but Miss Powell's cards felt different - heavier, older, as if they'd seen more than one lifetime.

There was so much to learn about the cards and the secrets they held.

After mixing them up herself, Miss Powell then asked Ella to take the cards and shuffle them whilst focusing on a question or area of her life. Ella was familiar with this ritual.

She mixed the cards and then cut them into three piles, before reassembling them into one. Sometimes she said her question out loud, but today she felt she wanted to keep it to herself.

She wasn't ready to share her experience behind the golden mirror just yet with Miss Powell or anyone else, for that matter. The question she'd focused on in her mind was 'Should I visit the world behind the mirror again?'

Miss Powell turned over the top card and Ella recognised it instantly. The Fool was a Major Arcana Card, and Ella focused on the picture. It was golden in colour and showed a young man with what would appear to be all his worldly belongings in a small knapsack over his shoulder.

Ella knew some of the meaning of this card. She knew that he had so little with him that he was not too worried about material things. He looks into the distance, seemingly unaware that he may be on the verge of stepping off a cliff. He seems almost serene.

'Ah,' said Miss Powell, 'this chap is telling me that you will be going on a journey soon and that you must be brave enough to step into the unknown.' Miss Powell looked closely at Ella.

'It is only by starting this journey that you can become clearer on what path you should take. The Fool is telling me that you must throw caution to the wind and not think too hard about what you are doing. He also tells me that there will be challenges on the way and many lessons to learn. Begin your journey and allow your Spirit to come through and guide you in the right direction.'

Wow, thought Ella. *That is so where I am at right now.* It could point to so many directions in my life at this time. Ella thought to herself about the journey she had just been on when she stepped through the golden mirror. She felt that this was the message she needed to hear to continue exploring the golden mirror experience again.

She pondered on what Miss Powell had just told her. She realised that she was sitting there, staring into space and not saying a lot. She had been feeling unsettled since her experience with the mirror, and this card confirmed that she was on the start of a journey.

She looked up to find Miss Powell looking at her. 'That card spoke to you, did it not, my dear? I can see the cogs and wheels working in your brain. I won't pull any more cards for you today. I think the Fool has said enough, and I can feel his energy all around.'

'Thank you, I think it's just what I needed to hear,' said Ella and Miss Powell smiled at her.

'No matter what the Fool says, do be mindful and don't get lost – be ready to guide yourself and listen to those who can mentor you through this journey that is ahead of you.'

'Of course.' Ella was wondering who those mentors might be.

Had she stepped through into another world and another time somehow, when she went through the golden mirror and created a sacred and magical space? She intended to find out.

Chapter 13

Ella thought about the many guided meditations and shamanic journeys she'd experienced over the years and believed that there are spirit guides on different planes that are there to guide and help us through the journey we call life.

The more she thought about it, the more she felt that Lily could be her spirit guide or a mentor from another dimension. It began to make sense to her to go back to the golden mirror and do precisely what she had done the first time, trying to get back into what she felt was an alternative world.

With her mind made up to retrace exactly what she had done before, she became excited at the thought of going on this adventure again. This time, she'd be better prepared and know more of what to expect.

Somewhere in the distance, she faintly heard the sound of her phone ringing. Ella was unsure what to do - part of her wanted to go up to the attic and go behind the golden mirror again, but another part of her thought she should answer her phone. She dithered a bit; mobiles always made things feel urgent, so she answered.

It was Janey. Darn, she had forgotten to message her to say she was not planning on meeting up with her tonight. 'We're upstairs in the pub.' The buzz of pub conversation could be heard in the background. 'We're just having a few drinks here and maybe picking up something to eat later. When are you going to be here?'

'Ah,' said Ella, 'I'm still at the house. I wasn't planning on...'

But before Ella got the chance to finish her sentence, Janey said, 'And don't bother telling me you're not coming. Guess who I bumped into earlier and said he is maybe going to come down – because you are?'

'I've no idea,' said Ella.

'Come on, Ella, how many guys do you know who are going to ask after you?' It was Scott, your handyman. I met him on the High Street earlier, and when I said you were coming for a drink and that he should come, he said he might pop down. See you soon,' Janey sang, and with that, she put the phone down, leaving Ella staring down at the phone in her hand.

Hmmm, explore the attic or have a drink down at the pub with the potential of seeing Scott? The thought of seeing Scott gave her the push to go meet up with everyone after all.

She had missed seeing him the day before, so this was her chance to make up for it. Maybe he did like her a wee bit after all.

She tidied herself up, put on some lipstick, let her hair out of its clasp and threw on her coat. Unknown to her, she looked great.

She popped her head into the sitting room. 'I'm off to meet Janey and a few others after all, Miss Powell. I won't be late.'

Miss Powell looked up from her book and said, 'Sounds like a journey you should make.' She smiled knowingly. 'Have a nice time and see you in the morning.' She returned to her book and Ella headed out. She hurried up the hill to catch the bus that was due. She got on and sat at the front upstairs, enjoying the view of Edinburgh on a quiet evening. She got off at the High Street and walked down the Royal Mile, admiring the beautiful old buildings. She loved seeing all the tourists and listening to the various languages spoken by people enjoying the evening. She'd always enjoyed the diversity of visitors in Edinburgh.

She arrived at The Waverley Bar, a cosy and famous spot for folk nights. Janey and her friends were there, but Scott was missing. Ella was a bit disappointed but tried to shrug it off.

She tried to tune into the group, but she was really lost in her own world. Janey nudged her. 'Dave's talking to you.' Janey turned to Dave with a cheeky wink. 'Don't worry about Ella, Dave, she just bobbles about in her own wee world, don't you, Ella?'

'Sorry, Dave, I never heard what you said.' She turned her attention to him,

CHAPTER 13

and he blethered on about the latest happenings in his world.

He didn't ask any questions about what was going on with her. Ella was pretty certain he was more interested in the sound of his voice and opinions than in listening to or learning anything about her.

Then that nagging voice in her head started to say - he probably doesn't ask anything about you because he thinks you're boring. She had to stamp on the negative voice in her head. She reminded herself that it was because she and Dave had nothing in common that she was finding the conversation boring and hard work.

But Ella wasn't a rude person, so she asked a few questions, listened to him and drank her wine until Janey decided that it was time to go and eat some food.

The group agreed, finished their drinks, put on their coats and got ready to go. *Perfect,* thought Ella, *I can slip away now.* 'I ate before I came out,' she fibbed, 'so I think I'll just head home now. It's been fun, thanks for asking me.'

'Are you sure?' asked Janey.

'Yeah, I'm sure. It's been nice to see everyone, but I'm off.' Janey hugged Ella and set off with her friends.

What a relief, Ella thought. *Now I can enjoy the rest of the evening.*

Chapter 14

Ella walked down St Mary's Street towards the Cowgate, a lively area full of hostels, hotels, clubs, pubs, and student accommodation. She passed Bannerman's pub on Niddry Street, where she'd spent many Saturday afternoons dancing to live bands. It was a grungy rock bar, but she loved that it was built within some of the mysterious Vaults beneath one of the city's main bridges.

Ella had always been fascinated by the dark history of old Edinburgh and knew a lot about the area, especially the vaults that lay beneath the bridges.

When the old bridge was built in the 1770s, connecting the New Town to the Old City, the builders, instead of filling in the large bases of the bridge, created a honeycomb of interconnecting cellars. Initially, these cellars were intended for merchants to use as store rooms, but they were too damp and dark. The merchants complained and demanded that the cellars be removed from their deeds so they wouldn't be taxed.

It didn't take long before some of Edinburgh's poor and homeless moved into the catacombs of cellars, making them their only shelter. They were a dreadful place to live - dark, damp, and heavy with the smell of rot. There was no sanitation, no running water, and no daylight.

The darkness also attracted the worst of people - thieves, rapists, even murderers - who quickly realised they could vanish into the depths of the catacombs and never be found.

For decades, this harsh life underground went on, until a massive fire ripped through The Vaults. No one knew how many men, women, and children had burned to their deaths. After that, the vaults became so filthy and overrun

CHAPTER 14

with rats and corpses that even the most desperate avoided them.

The 'Fathers of the City,' or what would be called the City Council today, decided to clear out the catacombs as best they could. Some cellars were filled with rubble to prevent flooding, and every entrance was blocked so no one could return – and, more spookily, so no one trapped inside could escape.

Eventually, the maze of catacombs was forgotten, becoming another shadowy part of Edinburgh's past.

Until, as the story goes, a man living on Niddry Street decided to do a little home improvement. He took a sledgehammer to one of his walls, expecting perhaps an extra few inches of space behind the plasterboard. Instead, his hammer broke through into nothingness. Intrigued, he removed the whole wall and stepped into a hidden cellar that hadn't been touched for hundreds of years.

One discovery led to another. The cellars became known as The Vaults, and a local businessman bought properties on Niddry Street and around the Cowgate. With permission to explore and renovate, he began creating bars and clubs underground. Just when he thought he'd mapped them all, he'd take down another wall and uncover yet another dark chamber.

In the early years, the Vaults became a popular rehearsal space for local bands, but some musicians left early and never came back – unnerved by strange noises or the prickling sensation of unseen eyes in the dark.

Nowadays, you can take a ghost tour beneath the city, straight into the vaults. But do be careful not to wander off – you might never be found again.

All this history whispered through Ella's mind as she wandered past Niddry Street. She could almost feel the damp chill rising from the cobbles, smell the faint tang of beer from the pubs, and sense the weight of centuries pressing down. She crossed into the Grassmarket and began walking up one of the most magical streets in Edinburgh – Victoria Street.

The cobbled curve led from the Grassmarket to George IV Bridge, its structure unchanged for hundreds of years. The colourful shopfronts kept the charm of old Edinburgh, and walking there always felt like stepping back in time.

At the top, Ella crossed the road to wait for her bus home. It wasn't long before it came. She climbed aboard, settled into her seat, and watched the city drift past. Closing her eyes, she dreamed about old Edinburgh – and all the stories it could tell.

Chapter 15

The next morning, Ella woke feeling refreshed and ready for the day ahead. She got up and put the kettle on for a pot of tea. Miss Powell had already had her breakfast, but Ella knew she would enjoy a cup at this time of the morning.

Balancing the tea tray, Ella nudged the living room door open with her foot.

'Morning,' she said.

'Morning, lass,' replied Miss Powell. 'It's going to be a lovely day today.'

Ella glanced out the window. The sky was a blanket of grey, but she had faith in Miss Powell's uncanny ability to read the weather.

'Good,' Ella said. 'I could do with a wee dose of sunshine.'

'The sun will come out a wee bit later this morning,' Miss Powell predicted.

'Look forward to it,' Ella smiled, pouring the tea and setting a cup and saucer beside Miss Powell.

'I was chatting to Mrs Donaldson yesterday,' Miss Powell began. 'You must know her - she lives in the house on the corner with the blue gate and fence. Always pottering about in her garden. She's lived here all her life, and she must be nearly ninety now, if not more. She's seen plenty of comings and goings in her time. You should go and see her if you want a history of the house from before I lived here.'

'That's a great idea. Did you mention I might be interested in chatting with her?' asked Ella.

'Aye, that I did, lass, and she'd be delighted to reminisce about old times with you.'

Perfect, thought Ella. It would be fascinating to hear what life was like here before Miss Powell moved in – and perhaps Mrs Donaldson might even remember who used to live in this house.

Ella munched her toast, gazing out into the garden where the trees swayed gently in the breeze.

Sundays were her day for deep-cleaning the kitchen and cooking dinners for the week ahead. Once she'd finished her tea, she carried the tray back to the kitchen and made a start on her day.

Chapter 16

Scott woke early on Sunday. Jobs were waiting for him, but he decided he'd see how he felt later. Sundays weren't for rushing.

He shuffled to the kitchen of his Pilton flat, made himself a coffee, and stood at the window. The sky was a pale wash of grey, but he didn't mind. It was good to wake up without a pounding head. He'd had too many Sundays that started with the sour taste of last night's mistakes.

As he sipped, his mind drifted back.

He'd grown up not far from here, in another council estate. It had been rough then - one of the worst reputations in Edinburgh - although regeneration had softened it in recent years. New flats stood where neglected blocks once loomed, a mix of single parents, young couples, students, and working families.

Back then, the three tower blocks dominated the estate. The one he lived in had twenty-three floors, and the lift rarely worked. Damp seeped through the walls, causing the wallpaper to peel within weeks. Some of the balconies, some of which had really nice sea views, were thick with pigeon droppings, and no one ever ventured out on them. Scott once saw a cockroach skitter across the kitchen floor. The heating was electric - too costly to put on, and even if it was put on, it was useless in the cold, damp flats.

Some flats became drug dens, steel doors bolted shut, deals done through letterboxes. Families avoided the towers, so big empty flats were handed to young people and single mums. It was a bad mix - party flats, rubbish-strewn stairs, the stench of urine, and broken bottles underfoot.

Kids had to run a gauntlet of gangs on the stairs to get home.

For some, it was terrifying. For Scott, it was just life.

There was still a sliver of community. Neighbours checked in on each other's kids. If a young mum hadn't been seen in a while, someone would knock on her door. But for Scott and his little brother, that safety net wasn't enough.

By the time Scott was a toddler, his mum was lost to alcohol and drugs. Valium to sleep, uppers to party, drink all day. She'd fallen out with her family as a teen and wanted nothing to do with them. Their father was never in the picture.

Motherhood, for her, had been an accident – but it got her a council flat and allowed her to escape her cruel stepfather. She saw her children more as obstacles than family. Weekends, she vanished – out clubbing, drinking, or disappearing with whichever boyfriend was around.

Sometimes she'd ask a neighbour to keep an eye on the boys. Sometimes she didn't bother. Either way, nothing would stop her from going out.

Scott learned quickly that if they were going to eat, he'd have to make it happen. He did what he could with whatever money or food was left. Schoolwork wasn't a priority – survival was.

Teachers never asked why he was falling behind. He didn't tell them. It was easier to hide behind a hard shell and pretend he didn't care. The truth was, the taunts about his ragged clothes and dirty face stung more than he'd care to admit.

By twelve, he'd stopped pretending. He skipped school, sniffed glue, and shoplifted. Eventually, the police caught him often enough that he and his brother were taken into care, but put into different care homes.

In some ways, the care home was better, with hot meals and clean clothes and somewhere safe to sleep. But safety was relative. Bullying still happened, and he learned to stand his ground or sink.

Trouble still found him. Juvenile detention – 'baby jail' – came next. He arrived streetwise, unwilling to be pushed around. With his brother locked up in a different centre across the city, they drifted further apart.

If the system aimed to set him straight, it failed. Inside, he picked up skills no teacher would give you – how to pick a lock, the going price for drugs, who

CHAPTER 16

to sell to, and who to buy from.

When he got out at sixteen, there was nowhere to go. His mum had lost her flat - years of unpaid rent caught up with her. She was living with yet another abusive boyfriend, somewhere nearby. Scott didn't care to find her. And she didn't care enough to find him.

It had been a rough start, no doubt. But it was his start. And it had made him who he was - resilient, guarded, and quietly determined never to need anyone again.

Chapter 17

That was how Scott found himself homeless on the cold streets of Edinburgh at sixteen. When he left the detention centre, he was hardy and stubborn, missing all his social work appointments and deciding to make his own way.

For about a year, he drifted – sleeping in various church graveyards in the city centre, begging on the streets, drinking cheap cider, stealing and reselling goods, and eating most days at soup kitchens. It became his life.

There were many outreach workers from homeless organisations who came around to help people sleeping rough. Some were okay, and Scott would sometimes chat and share a smoke with the more interesting ones to pass the time – but he refused any help. Eventually, most gave up on him.

Except Ruth.

She passed his favourite begging spot in the city centre every two or three days, just to see how he was doing. Something about her told Scott she'd been through a lot herself. She seemed to understand him without judging. He trusted her – a rare thing.

Ruth didn't push. She'd just say hello, have a cigarette with him, and chat. Every so often, she'd repeat the same words:

'When you're ready to move on, Scott, let me know, and I'll see what I can do to help.'

One day, begging on the Mound in the rain, Scott hit rock bottom. Hungover, hungry, sick, cold, wet, and filthy, he looked at Ruth and decided on the spot.

'Can you help me? I think I'm ready to move on.'

From there, Ruth moved quickly. Within two days, she got him into one of the better halfway houses in the city. He had to share a room with three

CHAPTER 17

others, but they were okay – they were trying, too.

Scott grabbed the opportunity with both hands. He'd met too many 'old-timers' on the streets who had been living that way for years, and he didn't want to end up like them. He cleaned himself up, got new clothes from the hostel, stopped drinking, and realised he needed something to keep him busy.

Ruth found him volunteer work at a furniture organisation, and Scott discovered he was good at fixing things. To his surprise, he enjoyed having somewhere to go every day and being around people from all walks of life. He found himself laughing and talking with people he never would have spoken to in the past.

His old mates would have called anyone who wasn't from a housing estate a 'snob.' Scott quickly learned that wasn't true. These volunteers didn't judge him, so he wasn't in a hurry to judge them.

With Ruth's help in navigating the maze of forms, Scott was offered a flat within a few months, in a newer, cleaner housing estate on the north side of the city. It was a mixed community: unemployed people, single parents, students, and working families. Some had bought their council houses years earlier, bringing pride and stability to the area.

Scott moved in with help from voluntary organisations he hadn't even known existed, including one that gave him a grant to cover his driving theory and practical tests. He passed within months. Ruth also showed him how to budget for bills, rent, council tax, and food – the kind of skills he should have learned in juvenile detention, but never did.

Life was finally taking shape.

At the furniture project, one of his fellow volunteers was an interesting older lady called Miss Powell. They got on like a house on fire. One day, she asked if he'd be interested in some paid handyman work at her home.

It was as if she saw his potential before he did. And so his own business, Scott Johnston, Handyman, was born.

That morning, sipping coffee, Scott thought about how far he'd come. He was proud of his life and business. He still saw familiar faces from his past, people who hadn't made it out.

He wondered if Ella had gone to the pub last night after all. Her sister

Janey had been insistent when they bumped into each other on the High Street that he join them. He'd said he'd try, but deep down he knew that after Ella's coolness during the week, he was more likely to head home than risk embarrassing himself again.

Stretching, he decided today was a good day to make some money. He texted a customer to say he'd be along later that morning to do some gardening.

Chapter 18

Meanwhile, on the other side of the city, Ella was knocking on a big blue door with a polished brass knocker, handle, and letterbox. Mrs Donaldson answered. She was a petite, plump elderly lady with silver hair, rosy cheeks, and a warm smile. She wore an apron over her dress and had a duster in one hand.

'Hello, Mrs Donaldson, I'm Ella and I work over at Miss Powell's house on the corner.'

'I know who you are, dear,' she said. 'Miss Powell tells me you're interested in the history of her house. Come in and I'll put the kettle on.' Mrs Donaldson settled Ella into her little sitting room and insisted on making tea. Ella sat in one of the two high-back chairs and gazed out at the beautiful garden, filled with springtime flowers.

Mrs Donaldson came in with a tray and poured them both a lovely cup of tea.

'It's very kind of you to spend some time with me,' said Ella.

Mrs Donaldson settled into a chair and began. 'When you get to my age, my dear, it is a pleasure to talk about my days as a young girl. So many happy memories of living here. I have lived here my entire life, and at 94, I have witnessed many changes in the area. I'll let Miss Powell tell you of her childhood and her memories of the house when she was growing up. She will tell it better than I.'

Mrs Donaldson paused, drifting away for a moment or two. 'Some of these memories come from my mother as well, because I was just a young lass at the time. But I do remember the family that used to live in the corner house -

the Frasers.' She sipped her tea.

'My mother told me that Mr Fraser was never quite the same after he returned from the First World War. You have to realise the war was very difficult, and many men were lost to it. Those who did come back - well, some were so traumatised they never got over it. It became known as shell shock, but during and after that war, people didn't have a name for it.'

Mrs Donaldson continued, 'My mother told me that Mr Fraser was such a gentleman before the war. But when he returned, he was a different man. Not physically ill, but in his head, he was still in the middle of the trenches.' She sighed.

'Poor Mrs Fraser was at her wits end with him and tried her best. Their daughter, who was a volunteer at the mental asylum at the time, tried to convince her father to see a doctor, but he wouldn't hear of it. You see, my dear, sadly, mental health carried a heavy stigma in those days. The daughter, though, was determined to help her father. She came home with a friend one day - a lovely lady - who started to work with Mr Fraser. From the stories we heard, with her magical herbs and tinctures, she helped Mr Fraser begin to recover. 'But,' Mrs Donaldson added mischievously, 'Miss Powell can tell you much more about her than me.'

How interesting, thought Ella. *What has Miss Powell got to do with that story?* She continued to listen intently, intrigued that the daughter of the house volunteered at the asylum.

She remembered that in her vision - or journey, or whatever it was - the young lady of the house had talked about her uniform for volunteering at the asylum. What a strange coincidence - or was it something more? She realised Mrs Donaldson was still chatting and pulled herself back into the present.

'There weren't that many houses around here at that time,' Mrs Donaldson went on. 'Just the four houses, including their corner house, and this row of houses. The rest was countryside at that time, and of course the big asylum up the road, and the workhouse the other way.'

'I remember the daughter - she was a lovely-looking lass. I didn't know her well, but those who did thought of her as a real powerhouse. Some said she

CHAPTER 18

was outspoken and outrageous for the times! When she made up her mind for something to happen, you could guarantee it would happen. Her mother was a much milder character whose life revolved around her husband.'

'Had they always lived in that house?' Ella asked.

'Now let me think,' pondered Mrs Donaldson. 'Yes, I remember hearing that the grandfather moved into the corner house when it was built, way back in Victorian times. The family lived there for years until Mr and Mrs Fraser moved to their country home down the Borders. I think the daughter stayed for a little while after they moved out, then the next family to move into the corner house was Miss Powell's family, when she was just a slip of a girl.'

Mrs Donaldson stopped to sip her tea. 'Dearie me, but I'm jumping ahead of myself.' She enjoyed having an avid listener to her memories.

Mrs Donaldson looked at Ella closely, as if seeing her for the first time. 'You know, now I look properly at you, the daughter looked a bit like you - you have the same hair and build. She was a tall and strong-looking lady. Maybe she's a distant cousin of yours. Wouldn't that be a funny thing?'

Mrs Donaldson chuckled, then her eyes widened as more memories returned. 'Now I remember - her name was Lily and...'

'Lily?' exclaimed Ella. 'Are you sure? ' She almost fell off her chair. It was the exact name of the woman she had met in her vision - or was it a journey? She wanted to hear more.

'Aye lass, I'm sure.' Mrs Donaldson was surprised by Ella's reaction. 'I always used to think it wasn't the right name for her because she was so un-Lily-like! A Lily is delicate and fair, and she was strong and dark! I recall hearing that she went on to work in the asylum, possibly as a nurse or even a doctor. It was very unusual in those days for a gentlewoman to become a working woman, but as I say, she was an unusual creature.'

Ella was intrigued. 'Do you remember anything else about Lily? She sounds like an interesting character for sure.'

'I know she got quietly married to someone who also worked at the asylum, and they moved out of the house shortly after. I remember seeing her a couple of times in the neighbourhood after that, visiting the new family in her old house. But I'm not sure where she ended up.'

Mrs Armstrong looked out into her garden, her mind reliving the past. A smile came over her face. 'Aye, Lily was a real character. A modern woman in an unmodern age. Whereas most women her age were worried about being left on the shelf and wanting to start a family, Lily was more interested in working and travelling.'

'I wonder if she had any children?' Ella wondered aloud.

'Oh, I don't know if she did. In those days, my dear, once someone moved out of the neighbourhood, there weren't ways of keeping up with people's news like nowadays. When someone left, you rarely saw them again unless they were family or very close friends.'

Ella couldn't believe the name was the same as the woman she had seen on her journey. Mrs Donaldson's description even sounded like her. This couldn't be a coincidence. Ella's mind went into overdrive trying to work it out.

She stopped herself from daydreaming and listened again.

Mrs Donaldson went on to tell Ella about other neighbours and houses in the street. She was a wealth of information, and Ella could tell she enjoyed reminiscing.

They finished their tea, and Ella thanked Mrs Donaldson, who assured her she had enjoyed their time together and invited her to visit again. Ella promised she would.

Standing outside, she decided to go for a walk to take in all she had just learned. Mrs Donaldson had also talked briefly about the old workhouse, which was in the opposite direction to the derelict asylum. It had been a while since she had walked that way. She hadn't known it was a workhouse - to her, it looked like an old hospital.

Intrigued to see it again through new eyes, she decided to walk up there. Mrs Donaldson had told her it was a workhouse for almost a hundred years. As times changed, the council took it over, and it became a home for the elderly in the 1940s called Greenlea.

In the 1980s, the old people's home was closed and sold to a developer, and the buildings were turned into expensive apartments.

Miss Armstrong had told her some of the old people had cried when they

CHAPTER 18

were told they were going to live in Greenlea, as some had been born into it when it was a workhouse.

As she walked through the serene neighbourhood, it was hard to imagine that some of the old buildings held such pain and suffering when they were homes for the poor and infirm.

Ella wandered about, clearing her head and thinking about what Mrs Donaldson had told her. How could it be that she knew the name of the girl who used to live in the house?

She returned to Miss Powell's house and busied herself with chores that didn't take much brainpower - she had so much to think about.

Chapter 19

The next morning, Ella woke with Mrs Donaldson's stories echoing in her mind. Was it just a coincidence that Lily, the asylum volunteer, shared the same name and was associated with the asylum, just like the woman from her strange journey? The thought sent a tingle of excitement through her, and although Ella still couldn't quite make sense of what had happened behind the mirror, she felt a strong pull to go back.

The more she turned it over in her mind, the more certain she became - it couldn't have been a dream. No, it had felt real, as though she'd stumbled upon a way to step into another, parallel world. She'd read stories, watched films about time travel, but could it be possible that she'd experienced it herself? Her thoughts buzzed with the unknown, and her head was full of questions she couldn't answer.

The next morning, Ella said goodbye to Miss Powell as she walked up the hill to get the bus. Every week, she went to Morningside to visit the library and then meet her friend for coffee.

Ella had a few tasks to do around the house, but since the house was empty, this was the perfect opportunity to return to the golden mirror and see if she could recreate her experience from the previous week.

Her pulse quickened and she couldn't ignore the tingle of excitement in her stomach as she made her way up the creaky old stairs to the attic, with its trunks, boxes and piles of papers. She had left the ring of old keys up there and knew the key that would turn the lock of the golden mirror. She put the key in the door, felt it slide open and pushed the door. Ella stepped in.

As she stood in the dark space, taking a deep breath, the air was cool and faintly scented with old dust and something faintly sweet, like dried flowers. She re-created her protection ritual around herself. She remembered the tarot card reading and the Fool card, which told her it was time to go on an adventure, but to be mindful as well.

She was ready! She did exactly what she had done the previous week and spun clockwise three times, took another deep breath, and gasped as everything around her felt as if it dissolved into a swirl of colours and sensations. The air around her crackled with a fiery energy, pulling her deeper into the unknown. She held onto the side of the cupboard to stop herself from falling. When the sensation stopped, she felt as if she had floated the cupboard and into the attic.

She looked around and was thrilled, and slightly scared, if she were to be honest with herself - the attic had been transformed again. It was still familiar, but it was filled with Victorian toys, clothes, and suitcases. She turned around and was prepared this time when she looked in the mirror. According to the mirror, she didn't exist - she had no reflection in this world.

Ella now knew that she had found a doorway into the past. Although she could not physically see herself, she could still feel her emotions and felt that her body was there, even though she could not see it.

She accepted that this was the way she was to move around in this world, and she experimented with her energy, directing it towards the wall, then back towards the mirror. She quickly grasped how to direct her energy where she wanted it and was ready to explore.

Chapter 20

Ella floated down the attic stairs and into the hall, wondering what to do and where to go, when she heard the bedroom door open. Lily walked out fully dressed in a sensible navy dress and coat that fell to her calves, and wore a simple navy hat, practical yet neat, with a small ribbon trim.

The last time Ella met Lily, she had put on lipstick and a spritz of perfume. Instead of perfume, there was only the faint smell of soap. Today, she could see that her face was freshly scrubbed and had no makeup on.

An older lady came through the door that Ella knew was the main living room. 'Oh, Lily, are you going up to that asylum again to volunteer?' The woman looked pained at the thought of it. Her brow furrowed, lips tightening as though she'd tasted something sour.

Ella took a good look at the lady. She was older, ranging in age from 50 to 60 years old. Her hair was a mix of grey and brown, pinned back quite severely. She wore a white and green floral dress that fell to her calves, and she had a string of short pearls around her neck, along with a gold wedding ring. Brown stockings and sensible black, flat shoes completed her outfit.

'A young lady like you should be doing nice things like drawing or painting, perhaps, so when you meet a nice young man, you'll have some skills to show off,' the woman said, pausing to catch her breath before continuing. 'I don't like how much time you spend at that dreadful asylum with all those...' She hesitated, searching for the right word. '...strange patients. Surely, some of them must be dangerous. You think you're being helpful, but more than likely, you're just getting in the way.'

Ella watched the two of them closely. This older woman had to be Lily's

CHAPTER 20

mother - an older, wearier version of her. The resemblance was unmistakable, although life had taken its toll on her. Her eyes, though the same shade as Lily's, seemed dulled by years of worry.

'Oh, Mother,' Lily said with an exasperated sigh, adjusting her hat as she prepared to leave. 'If only you could meet some of the patients. They're not all strange or dangerous - they're ill, and they need help. Your attitude is so outdated. It's the 1920s! If the war taught us anything, it's that women are just as capable as men of working and making a difference in the world.'

She straightened her coat and continued, her frustration coming out. 'Just because the war is over doesn't mean women should go back to being seen and not heard. And for the record, my work at the asylum is appreciated.'

Lily sighed, speaking more to herself than her mother now. 'Though I know the office work is important, I'd much rather be helping directly with the patients. I know I could be far more useful in the wards. Maybe one day,' she added wistfully, a flicker of determination in her voice. Her chin lifted, eyes bright with determination.

'Don't let your father hear you say such things. Even a whisper of the war sets him off. It's stayed with him, changed him... he's not quite the man he was before, and he doesn't understand what you're doing,' said her mother sadly, glancing back at the door that she had just come through.

'It is exactly why I feel so strongly about volunteering and trying to help at some level, people whose lives were shattered by the war. A lot of those so-called strange patients, as you called them, are men who have been traumatised by what they saw during the war, not unlike Father. They are encouraged to work in the grounds, have fresh air, and talk to the special doctors.' Lily was not to be stopped; she continued, tired of her mother having a go at her.

'By volunteering at the hospital, at least I feel that I am doing something useful with my time. And just so you know, I am not interested in learning some hobbies so that I can please some man in the future.'

A deep, loud and angry voice came from the direction of the drawing-room. 'Dora? Where the hell are you? I need you here. Now.' The voice cracked through the air like a whip, startling even Ella.

'Oh dear,' said Lily's mother, 'your father needs me and needs you too, Lily. You should be helping me look after your father, not looking after strangers and disgracing yourself and this family by lowering yourself through volunteering. I mean, what do our neighbours think?'

'First of all, mother, I don't care what the neighbours think. If they can't see the good in helping others less fortunate than themselves, then I don't want anything to do with them. Secondly, Father has you and Alison running after him all day long. He certainly doesn't need any more help from me.' Lily decided it was time for her mother to hear her opinions, so she took a deep breath and continued.

'I understand that he is suffering from the trauma of the war, but doing everything for him is not the way to help him, at least I don't think so.'

Lily looked at her mother and said firmly, 'It would do him the world of good to get out into the garden, or his woodshed, and do something more pleasant with his time. He was a talented woodworker who also loved drawing and painting. It would be so good for him to get lost in a hobby, rather than being left to sit with nothing to do, allowing his memories to trick him into thinking he is still in the war.'

Despite her harsh words, Lily felt very sad for her father. He was a completely different man since he returned from the war. He had fought in the trenches in France during World War I. Lily had heard enough stories from the asylum, from men on the front, to know some of the horrors that her father and others had seen and endured.

Lily tried to get her mother to encourage him to do something different with his day instead of just sitting in his chair. She didn't blame her mother for not trying something different; her mother was living in fear of saying the wrong thing to her husband and starting a tyrant of abuse aimed at her.

She was opting for the safe and reliable option of doing everything for him, not realising that this probably wasn't the best way forward.

Lily admired the asylum's policy, which encouraged patients who were suffering from the terrible things they had witnessed during the war. Some doctors suggested that patients spend time doing the type of activity they had previously enjoyed before becoming ill or before the war, particularly for

CHAPTER 20

many of the male patients.

The board of doctors and directors generally believed that maintaining a busy schedule with familiar activities was a significant step in our improvement. Although, sadly, some doctors in the asylum shunned ideas like those and preferred the treatment of drugs, locking patients up and using restraints to stop patients from talking or moving about.

Lily remembered her father before he was recruited into the army. He was a man of few words, but she knew he loved her. He enjoyed his work at the printers in Fountainbridge, just a short distance from their home. Her father was greatly liked and was known at his work for being a fair boss. He would often bring her mother home a flower or some small gift, and they would sit and chat for hours in the garden, at peace with the world and themselves.

Her father would happily give a helping hand to any of his friends or neighbours and was a real gentle soul. The war had triggered something in his mind that he couldn't shake off, and he now suffered from nightmares, was angry and confused by his surroundings, and his hearing was far less than it used to be.

Lily wished her father would allow her to help him. If he would, she would take him out of the house and do something else apart from shouting at her mother, making demands on Alison the housemaid, staring into space and keeping on recounting the horrors that he saw in the war.

Lily sighed, realising that today, she couldn't do anything to help her father, and made her way out of the house and towards the grounds of the asylum. The air outside was brisk, carrying with it the faint scent of damp earth and the distant clang of the asylum gates.

Chapter 21

The asylum, or hospital as Lily preferred to call it, had opened its doors to women volunteers during the war, and they had proved themselves to be invaluable to the asylum's operation.

Ella was excited about the prospect of seeing the asylum in its heyday. She had daydreamed about what life would have been like there many times as she walked around the old, disused buildings and grounds, and was fascinated by the old buildings, their varied uses, and the people who had once lived in them. Being here in a different period when it was in use and alive with people was exciting for her.

Ella felt her energy merge with Lily's, allowing her to see the world through her eyes while still holding onto her own thoughts. It was an unsettling but fascinating sensation – like slipping into a borrowed coat, warm but not quite fitting – being part of someone else's body and thought process.

Lily walked past the vegetable garden, her steps purposeful as she approached the main building. Ahead, the grounds were scattered with patients – some seated on benches, others on chairs, while a few wandered aimlessly, lost in their own worlds.

Ella could hear a few patients talking to themselves – some more animated than others – and occasionally she would hear a scream or shout from another part of the grounds. The tang of damp soil hung in the air, mixed with the faint smell of coal smoke drifting from a chimney somewhere nearby.

Lily walked towards the building, but not towards the grand main entrance. She entered through a small door on the side of the building and stepped into a room that looked like an office.

CHAPTER 21

The room had two tables in it, and one was overflowing with papers and files. There were a couple of tall cupboards with lots of drawers, perhaps an old-fashioned filing system, thought Ella.

Lily took off her coat and sat down at one of the desks, immediately starting to sort through the papers and files.

The room was heavily panelled with wood and had a large rug in the middle as well as a fireplace with a grand mantelpiece surrounding it. The room had two big windows looking out over the grounds. From the windows, another building could be seen and beyond that, the ancient woodland. Soft daylight streamed through the glass, casting pale patterns across the rug. It was a lovely view.

Ella focused on removing her energy from Lily so she could float around more freely. She couldn't help but be disappointed. She had been hoping that Lily would walk through the corridors of the hospital so that she could get a sense of what life was like in the asylum a hundred years ago.

She was beginning to wonder if she should go and explore herself when she was distracted from her thoughts by the door being opened by a tall, thin man in a white coat.

He stepped into the office and closed the door behind him. The smell of antiseptic and an overpowering whiff of hair oil accompanied him. With him, the atmosphere of the room changed. Lily looked up when she heard the door.

'Dr Ramsey,' she said coldly, 'can I help you?' *Ooh*, thought Ella, she could tell by the tone of Lily's voice that she did not like this man one little bit.

Dr Ramsey moved closer to Lily. His hair was almost black, slicked back with some kind of hair oil. He was not a pleasant-looking man at all. He had a thin face, mean lips, ice-cold blue eyes and an air of arrogance around him.

As he moved closer, Lily tried to push her chair away from him. He came uncomfortably close to her and put a hand on her shoulder. His touch seemed to carry a clammy, unwanted weight. 'Ah, Lily, you know I always like to come and see you when you are here.' He had a guttural, thick Scottish accent.

Ella watched from the corner of the room. She could feel how uncomfortable Dr Ramsey made Lily feel. Lily stood up from her desk, forcing the Doctor to step away.

'I've asked you before, Dr Ramsey,' Lily said coldly as she stepped as far away as she could from him. 'Do not stand so close to me, or put your hand on my shoulder. I am here in my capacity of office volunteer, although you know that I would be of much better use in the wards, actually working alongside the nurses and patients.'

'Ah, yes,' said Dr Ramsey. 'A word or two from me to the board and I'm sure we could reposition you.'

He looked Lily up and down in a smarmy way. 'Perhaps you should reconsider my offer of marriage to you, Lily. After all, another year or two, and you will be considered an old spinster and no good to anyone. It's not every girl that gets an offer of marriage from a prestigious doctor of psychiatry,' he said smugly, 'and my offer won't be on the table forever. Imagine the prestige you would have as an esteemed doctor's wife. You could take on any position in the asylum, well, the highest position a woman as a volunteer can have, I should say.' He sniggered at the thought of a woman in a high position – it was a ridiculous notion to him.

At that moment, the door opened again, and a large woman dressed in a black uniform with a practical white apron over it, with a white cap, came into the room.

'Dr Ramsey, excuse me for interrupting,' with a look on her face that said nothing of the kind, 'but you are needed in ward 12.'

'Yes, Matron, I will be there momentarily. I shall finish my business with Lily here in the office.'

The Matron looked at Lily and said, 'If there is anything I can help you with, Lily, you only need to ask, and then you don't need to bother the doctor.'

'Thank you, Matron, but you did a good job when you showed me how I could help organise this office when I started. I didn't ask Dr Ramsey to come into this office at all, and he has yet to discuss any official business. Believe me, as far as I am concerned, he can leave right now.' Lily stared directly at Dr Ramsey, challenging him to say anything else.

The Matron was an older woman who wore her uniform with pride, and it was clear that she was not someone who would be told what to do easily.

CHAPTER 21

She was formidable-looking and appeared to be very much in charge, but in a comforting way. There was a quiet strength in her stance, as if she could steady an entire ward simply by walking into it. The way she looked at Dr Ramsey made Ella think that Matron did not hold Dr Ramsey in high regard either.

'As I said, Doctor, you are needed elsewhere, and I suggest that you leave Lily to get on with her work. She is kind enough to do the work as a volunteer. Thank you, Lily.' Matron smiled at her.

She turned to look directly at Dr Ramsey until it was obvious that she wasn't leaving until Dr Ramsey did too.

He reluctantly moved away from Lily and allowed the Matron to usher him out. 'Yes, Matron. I understand that there are things in this asylum that only a senior doctor can deal with,' he said haughtily.

Before he closed the door, he turned to Lily and said, 'Do consider what I said, Lily. Good day to you,' and with that, he left with the Matron.

Lily gave a huge sigh of relief and sat down at her desk.

Ella admired the way Lily and the Matron had dealt with the Doctor. It would take a fair bit of guts to stand up to a man in those days, especially a man in power.

What a creep he is. Thank goodness Lily hadn't been taken in by him, or so desperate to marry that she would put up with anything or anyone!

Chapter 22

Ella enjoyed her time with Lily but wanted to return to her own life and time. It was a short walk home for Lily, and she was soon back at her house. Ella silently said goodbye to Lily and floated up the stairs into the attic, resisting the urge to drift through the rest of the house to see what was happening.

She began to feel a little anxious about her return to her own world. What if she got lost in time? Much as she was enjoying exploring Lily's world, she did not want to stay there. The thought sent a small shiver up her spine. She was excited about returning to her world and getting on with her life.

Determined to return to her own time and place, she focused her energy on moving through the mirror door, and when inside, she spun around three times clockwise.

When she felt the world stop moving around her, she took a deep breath and reached out to push the mirror door open. Her fingers tingled against the cool metal of the doorknob, instead of just being invisible energy.

She pushed the door open, stepped out, and looked around. Relief washed over her as she spotted the familiar bits and pieces in Miss Powell's attic. She turned around, and there in the mirror was her reflection. She pressed her nose, just to make sure she was real, and felt it squash against her finger.

Yep, she was back in her own time. What a journey! She sat on one of the old trunks to catch her breath and to digest what had just happened.

She was full of admiration for Lily. She seemed to know exactly what she wanted to do in life and had a clear idea of what was right and wrong. She was not going to let discrimination against being a woman stop her from getting the career she wanted –and most importantly of all, she put that creepy doctor in his place.

Yes, Lily was exactly the type of mentor Ella needed in her life. She was sure she could learn a lot from her.

She remembered the tarot card reading that Miss Powell had given her, specifically the Fool card, which told her to take heed of any new guides or mentors on her journey. The memory of the card's image flashed vividly in her mind - a figure standing at the edge of a cliff, ready to step into the unknown. She felt certain she could learn a great deal from a strong woman like Lily.

What a curious day. Who knew her mentor would be a woman who had lived almost a hundred years before her?

Ella lay on her bed and relived every detail - the scents, the sounds, the strange weightless feeling of moving between worlds. Somehow, she had found a portal into another world from around one hundred years ago.

What should she do now? Should she tell someone about it?

Would Miss Powell understand, or even believe her? She wished she could tell Scott -now that would be an interesting conversation.

Ella was pretty sure she wouldn't tell her sister Janey. Janey would be nosy, intrusive, and somehow cause trouble. For the time being, Ella decided to keep her journey to another time entirely to herself.

Chapter 23

Miss Powell had enjoyed her morning at the library and meeting up with her old friend, and now, having returned, was enjoying a peaceful afternoon, reading her newspaper and listening to the soft rustle of leaves outside, mingled with the cheerful chirping of birds in the garden. She heard Ella come down the stairs from the attic and wondered what she had been doing up there.

Miss Powell loved this house and had done so since she had moved there as a young girl. Her love of herbs and tarot cards came from her mother, who hailed from a long line of Romany people – some would call them gypsies.

Her mother had shocked her Romany family by marrying someone from outside their community, and her family moved on, leaving her to her new life. Losing her family had not been easy.

Her father was ostracised by his family for what they called 'tainting' the family name by marrying a gypsy. They were both disowned and only had each other. Still, they never regretted their union, as they loved each other deeply.

Miss Powell's mother, whose name was Rose, settled into her new life and tried to leave her Romany roots behind for the sake of her marriage. John, her husband, had never asked her to do so. He loved her so much that all he wanted was her happiness.

Miss Powell remembered her happy childhood. Before they lived in this big house, they had a small flat on the Southside of Edinburgh. It wasn't long before Rose's neighbours got an inkling of her talents with herbs and tinctures. Those who were curious watched as Rose collected plants from all around the neighbourhood, healing the sick with her potions whenever possible.

Initially, there were mixed reactions, but because Rose was such a lovely, kind, and gentle soul, she soon won people over. She became known for reading tea leaves and helping people see their situations more clearly with her tarot cards – the very same deck that Miss Powell used today.

Word spread about Rose's readings, and their home always seemed to have someone sitting around the table with her. It became an unspoken custom for friends and neighbours to bring something in return for a reading – a loaf of freshly baked bread, a pot of homemade jam, or, for those who could afford it, a coin or two.

Miss Powell remembered how her mother would take her to Arthur's Seat or local parks, and sometimes further afield to the outskirts of the city, to harvest special plants and herbs, leaves, nuts, berries, and fruit, depending on the season. Ella could almost picture it – Rose's hands brushing through tall grass, the earthy scent of damp soil clinging to the roots they pulled.

Rose would bring the bounty back to the little flat, drying out leaves and plants, and blending certain herbs into remedies. She had learned about the medicinal power of plants from her grandmother and mother, having grown up moving from place to place.

They also said Rose had healing hands. When someone had pain, she would lay her hands on the affected part, and a warmth would spread, easing tension like sunlight melting frost.

People like Rose, with deep knowledge of herbs and plants, were often known as folk healers and were valued in their communities, though some remained suspicious, even calling them witches.

In those days, there were no free doctors for the poor in Scotland. The National Health Service wouldn't come into existence until 1948, so a local healer with such skills was a true asset.

For Rose, helping others came naturally. It wasn't unusual for her husband, John, to come home and find a roomful of people waiting to see her. Even after working hard all day, he never complained. He was simply happy that his beautiful wife was happy.

John was originally from Leith, a large port that was its own town until merging with Edinburgh in the 1920s. He began as a clerk for a shipping company and, over the years, advanced within it.

The big bosses noticed his hard work, fairness, and honesty. He had a sharp sense for where shipments should go, which merchants to trust, and who would pay the most for incoming goods.

When his father died in the 1920s, John inherited a small sum - the result of a lifetime of scrimping and saving. He invested it in a small shipping company started by a friend. For years, it yielded little until the company secured a wartime contract to deliver goods to troops overseas. Known for delivering full cargoes without anything going missing, the company flourished.

John's investment paid off, and knowing he wanted children and a house with a garden, he saved steadily.

Born in 1899, John had suffered scarlet fever as a boy. When called up for the First World War, much to his mother's relief, he was turned down on medical grounds.

John was disappointed; like most young men of his time, he wanted to fight for his country. But many of his young friends did not ever return, and those that did returned from France broken - some with horrific injuries, others haunted by the invisible scars of what would later be called shell shock. Those memories stayed with him, casting a quiet shadow over even his happiest moments.

Chapter 24

Rose was horrified by the effects of shell shock. She had seen firsthand how the war could turn a hard-working, family loving man into nothing but a hollow shadow of his former self.

Often, the men returning from the war were angry, frustrated, and unable to express how they felt. They had witnessed unspeakable horrors up close - the kind that clung to them like a permanent shadow. When Rose looked into their eyes, she could see the haunted look of men who had experienced and seen things no one should ever have to see.

Rose worked tirelessly with shell-shocked men as they trickled back into her neighbourhood after the war. She felt they had been forgotten by the army, sent back home as if they could simply pick up where they had left off. But the war had taken pieces of them - some physical, some invisible - leaving wounds far deeper than anyone could see.

Many wives in the neighbourhood sent their husbands Rose's way, hoping she could help them.

Rose worked hard to awaken the long lost and carefully guarded knowledge she had learned from her grandmother and mother about specific plants and herbs. She consulted her tarot cards and then went out, crossing muddy paths or walking over shaded woodlands, searching, harvesting, and gathering plants and herbs from near and far.

She made tinctures and teas, encouraging the men to take them, but most importantly, she spent time with each person she worked with. She listened to them, letting them pour out their grief and frustration without judgement, and encouraged them to try new hobbies or, when they were ready, to find work they could manage.

The results were worth every ounce of her effort. Many of her patients began to change slowly; they lost their anger and frustration and started to accept that they could not change what they had seen. Instead, they began to look towards their families, their friends, and the possibility of a new life ahead.

With time and patience, some of the most shell-shocked men emerged from their depression and anger, beginning to heal and reconnect with the world around them.

Rose's work with war veterans became something of a local legend.

This was the environment Miss Powell had grown up in and was gathering herbs and making teas and tinctures from the time she could walk beside her mother. She learned how to read tea leaves and tarot cards at a young age.

They were a happy family, content with their lives, and Rose was always ready to help others. Miss Powell remembered her magical childhood fondly - the warmth of her parents' love, the scent of drying herbs filling the small kitchen, and the soft lamplight casting long shadows over the table as her mother shuffled her tarot deck.

Miss Powell brought herself back into the present. She looked out at the trees in the distance and listened to the wood pigeons cooing softly in the background.

She enjoyed thinking about times gone by. She had been pleasantly surprised when Ella started asking about the house's history, but she was reluctant to share her own story.

In time, she would - if Ella proved to be the right person to share it with. Mrs Donaldson had told Miss Powell that Ella had almost jumped out of her seat when she mentioned that a lady called Lily used to live here.

Why did Ella recognise that name? Lily had been a major player in changing her family's fortunes during her mother and father's lives back in the 1940s. How could a slip of a girl from nowadays know anything about Lily?

Miss Powell closed her eyes and allowed herself to drift back in time once more, recalling the story of how her mother and Lily had first met.

Chapter 25

Edinburgh's South Side in the 1920s was a grim place to be, especially compared to some of the more affluent parts of the city. There were streets and streets of tenements- or, as some called them, slums.

The area was full of thousands of families living alongside shops, cafés, and pubs, and there was even a cinema on Nicholson Street. Many families lived in each tenement, sometimes with eight or nine people crammed into one small flat. With a toilet on every other landing and no running water, living there was a real challenge- but none of them knew any different.

Electric lights were almost non-existent in this part of the city. Families relied on gas lamps and coal fires, making the flats smoky, tinged with soot, and carrying the scent of coal dust in the air.

However, one thing these areas did have in common was community. If a child scraped a knee or a family ran short of bread, there was always someone willing to help. Everyone mostly looked out for each other.

It was here that Miss Powell's parents lived, and where she was later born. Her mother, Rose, practised herbal medicine from her tiny flat and, for many years, did so with a baby to care for. She never turned anyone away, no matter how tired she was.

These were hard times. There wasn't much money for new clothes or shoes. Families wore garments until they fell apart, and shoes would be taken to the cobbler again and again until they simply couldn't be patched up anymore.

It was in this unlikely environment that Lily and Rose met.

One day, much like any other, Rose was at home mixing herbs, preparing tinctures, and tidying the flat when there was a knock at the door. That was unusual- most of her neighbours felt comfortable enough to walk right in if the door wasn't already open.

'Coming,' said Rose, wiping her hands. She opened the door to find, standing in the dim stairwell, a tall, beautifully dressed, dark-haired lady.

Her hair was cut in the latest short bob, her clothes fashionable and perfectly tailored. To Rose, she looked like she had stepped straight out of a magazine illustration.

This was certainly no neighbour.

'Oh, hello,' said Rose, momentarily taken aback. 'Can I help you? Gosh, where are my manners- do come in.'

Her first thought was that she might be in trouble. Was this woman from some official body looking to stop her from handing out herbal remedies? She had heard that the local doctor called her a quack- words she suspected her friends softened when repeating to her- and that he discouraged his paying patients from visiting her.

The fine-looking lady stepped into the wee flat. 'Hello. My name is Lily- Lily Fraser. I do apologise for just showing up on your doorstep, but I was so very keen to meet you.'

Rose blinked, wondering why on earth this elegant stranger wanted to meet her.

'I hope you don't mind, but I asked around the neighbourhood to find out where you lived,' Lily continued, smiling- a genuine smile that reached her eyes. 'Almost everyone knew who I was looking for, so you were easy to find.'

Rose moved a few clothes and other bits from the wooden chairs by the fire. 'Please, have a seat,' she said, 'and excuse the guddle!'

Lily sat down and took in her surroundings. She had never been in a tenement flat before. The sink stood in one corner beside a large wardrobe cupboard. The coal fire was the heart of the room, with a pot bubbling away on the stove, filling the air with an earthy, aromatic warmth.

A large dining table in the corner was covered with a tablecloth and dishes. Curtains hung over the recessed bed area where Rose and her husband slept.

But what drew Lily's attention most were the shelves lining two walls- crowded with bottles and jars in every shape and size, some filled with liquids,

CHAPTER 25

others with dried herbs. Hanging from the ceiling was a frame with wire mesh, and laid across it were plants and flowers left to dry. On another wall, bunches of herbs hung upside down.

It was a room like no other Lily had seen – a healer's workshop and a humble living space.

Realising she'd been staring, Lily said, 'Gosh, excuse me – I'm just taking in all the plants you have drying here. They look so interesting, and the room smells wonderful.'

Rose smiled, relieved that the woman seemed more interested in the herbs than in the cramped space.

Lily leaned forward. 'Let me tell you why I'm here. I volunteer at the asylum in Craighouse, in the south of the city. I'm very interested in alternative treatments, and when I heard stories of your incredible healing with herbs and tinctures, I wanted to meet you in person.'

Rose's shoulders eased. 'So, I'm not in trouble then. That's a relief.'

Lily shook her head. 'No of course, no! I've only heard good things about your practice.'

Rose still didn't quite understand why this elegant woman had sought her out until Lily began to tell her story.

She spoke of her father and how concerned she was for him. Since returning from the First World War many years ago, he had changed completely – still locked in a state of shock and trauma. He refused to leave the house or seek help. Her mother, Lily explained, walked on eggshells around him, never knowing when his temper might flare.

From her time at the asylum, Lily knew the signs of shell shock, and she had begun to hear stories of a healer on the other side of Edinburgh – someone who had helped other ex-soldiers.

'And that is why I am here,' said Lily. 'I want to ask you to come to my house and see my father.'

Rose hesitated. 'I'm glad you've heard good things, but I just help those who come to my door – neighbours and maybe friends of friends. I don't often leave the flat unless it's foraging for herbs. But it's kind of you to think I could help.'

What Rose did not yet know was that Lily was not a woman who took 'no' easily.

'I understand, but please - I will make it worth your while. I'll pay you for your time and any herbs you think may help. I can drive, and I could pick you up and take you back.'

Most of the people Rose helped couldn't pay her at all. The offer of payment - and a ride in a motor car to a different part of the city - was too tempting.

Rose thought for a moment. 'I can't promise anything, but if I can help, I will.'

'Wonderful,' Lily said. 'Shall I pick you up on Wednesday at around eleven?'

'That should be fine,' Rose replied.

As they shook hands, Lily felt a connection she rarely experienced. She knew, without doubt, that Rose was going to become an important part of her life.

Chapter 26

The next morning, Ella woke, her mind already drifting to Lily and the strange connection she felt to the world beyond the golden mirror. She glanced around her surroundings, checking that she was indeed in her own world, and let out a breath of relief. Yes, she was home.

As she stretched, a sense of calm settled over her. She felt light and hopeful, as though the world was full of endless possibilities waiting just for her. It still felt unreal – almost impossible – that she had stumbled upon a portal to another time. Yet, somehow, she had.

She admired Lily, who seemed to know exactly what she wanted from life, spoke her mind, and wasn't the type of person to let others control her. Ella thought there was so much she could learn from a woman like that.

She got up, dressed, and headed to the kitchen. She made a pot of tea and carried the tray into the living room, where Miss Powell sat gazing wistfully out the window.

Ella set the tray down, poured two cups, and settled onto the sofa. Miss Powell hardly seemed to notice her.

'Here's your tea, Miss Powell,' Ella said, handing her the cup and saucer.

'Oh my,' Miss Powell replied, 'I was drifting away.'

'Aye, I could see that,' said Ella. 'What were you thinking about?'

'I was thinking about how nice it would be to nurture our herb garden and start using it more often. What do you think?'

Ella tilted her head. 'I think that would be lovely. I've been pottering about in that part of the garden quite a lot recently. It's my favourite spot when I'm outside. It is pretty neglected and overgrown, and I don't know all the plants growing there – that's for sure. I tend to focus on the weeds in between the plants,' she added with a small laugh, 'but I'd love to learn more about them and give that area some love.'

'Let's see what the cards say, shall we?' Without waiting for an answer, Miss Powell reached for the purple silk bag, took out the tarot cards, held them against her heart, and closed her eyes.

'This reading is for both of us,' Miss Powell said mysteriously, handing Ella the deck. 'You know what to do.'

Ella took the beautifully worn cards in her hands, feeling their familiar weight and quiet hum of energy. She split the deck where it felt right, placed the cards into three piles, then combined them back into one.

Miss Powell took the deck, her movements deliberate, and turned over the first card: The Sun. A childlike figure rode a white horse beneath a glowing sun, surrounded by tall sunflowers under a clear sky.

'In this reading,' Miss Powell began, her voice steady and thoughtful, 'The Sun represents you. You're a beacon of positivity, someone who wants to bring light into the lives of others. Deep down, you long to open your arms to the world and declare, *this is who I am*! You're on a journey of self-discovery – learning who you are and what you truly want to do. Yes, there will be challenges, but you have an inner faith that things will work out. The Sun is a card of growth, optimism, and possibility.'

Ella absorbed the words, feeling a flicker of excitement stir inside her.

Miss Powell turned over the second card and smiled. 'Ah, The Page of Pentacles.' The image showed a young figure in a field, holding a pentacle with a focused, studious expression.

'This is a card of curiosity, learning, and discovery. You're standing at the threshold of understanding more about yourself and Mother Earth. Now is the time to decide – do you want to step onto this path and truly explore it?'

Finally, she turned over The Empress. A regal woman sat in a lush garden, surrounded by symbols of fertility and abundance.

'The Empress is a card of beauty and the cycles of nature. She embodies the nurturing, regenerative power of the Earth – her seasons, her growth, all she provides. This card reminds us of life's richness and the importance of

CHAPTER 26

connecting with nature.'

Ella studied the images. She longed to be like The Sun – open and confident – while deepening her connection to the Earth.

Miss Powell placed the cards down gently. 'This reading tells me you're ready – ready to dive deeper into what Mother Nature has to offer. You have the potential to be an excellent student of her ways.'

Ella leaned forward. 'What are you saying?'

Miss Powell smiled. 'If you're interested, we could begin an apprenticeship of sorts. You could start by tending the herb garden and learning the many ways plants can heal and nurture.'

'Wow!' Ella's face lit up. 'I'd love that. Can you teach me?'

'Oh yes,' Miss Powell said warmly. 'I'd be delighted. I've been waiting for the right student for a long time, and I was beginning to think my knowledge might pass with me. But lately, I've sensed you're ready. If you are truly interested, we can begin tomorrow.'

'I am,' Ella said quickly, wanting to reassure her.

She finished her tea, her mind buzzing with possibilities. As she went about her day, cleaning the house and tending her duties, her happiness only grew. For the first time in a long while, she felt she could see a clearer path ahead.

Later, she wandered into the garden, drawn to the herb patch with a fresh sense of wonder. She recognised some plants by their scent and shape, but so many were strangers to her. The thought of learning their secrets made her heart race. Tomorrow couldn't come soon enough.

Chapter 27

As she stood in the garden, she heard the garden gate creak open. Turning around, she saw Scott walking in, carrying a ladder. He propped it against the side of the house, and, as far as Ella was concerned, her day had just got brighter.

'Hey,' said Scott, 'how's it going?'

Scott was determined not to let himself get distracted by Ella today. He had decided they would be a casual kind of friend - not the kind you sat with for deep, world-fixing conversations, and certainly not a girlfriend. Just someone you said hi to, then got on with your day. Wishing for anything else, he told himself, was a waste of time. He figured it out - she wasn't interested in him.

'Hey, Scott,' said Ella.

She, on the other hand, had other ideas. She'd already learned a few life lessons from Lily, the strong woman from another century, and she was ready to take a chance. Pulling herself out of her daydream, she met Scott's gaze. She could easily get lost in his deep blue eyes, and the way the ladder rested against his shoulder showed off the muscles in his arms and shoulders. He looked good - and she could feel a tingle in her stomach just being near him.

Taking a deep breath, she decided it was time to let him know she'd like to get to know him better.

But before she could speak, Scott said, 'Can't be hanging about today, Ella. I've got a few jobs to get on with, and a hot date tonight.'

He glanced into her eyes - and for a second, he wondered if he'd just seen a

CHAPTER 27

flicker of disappointment there.

She did look good this morning: tousled hair, blue jeans, and a fitted tee. *Jeez,* he thought, *that girl would look good in rags.* But Scott had slipped into self-protective mode. Pretending he had a hot date seemed safer than letting her think he might be sitting at home, thinking about her. He'd learned young not to show his true feelings – a shield against being hurt.

'Oh,' Ella said, forcing a smile, 'sounds fun. You must let me know how it goes.'

She smiled outwardly, but inside, she felt gutted. In truth, she didn't care how the date went. *Lucky girl,* she thought, *whoever she is.*

Silly me, she told herself, *to think that a guy like him would be interested in me.* Negative thoughts crept in fast, whispering that she wasn't good enough.

She turned her back so he couldn't see her disappointment and busied herself in the herb garden. Behind her, she heard the clink of tools and the thud of his boots on the ladder rungs.

But the garden no longer felt like the refuge it had moments before. She was surprised at just how disappointed she felt. As she stood there, letting herself feel the sting, she realised something she hadn't fully admitted before – she liked him a whole lot more than she'd allowed herself to believe.

So much for me taking the plunge and telling Scott how I felt.

The day stretched ahead, and she'd already finished her housework. Tomorrow she would begin her herb lessons with Miss Powell – and that, at least, gave her something bright to look forward to.

Chapter 28

Ella's thoughts drifted to life on the other side of the mirror. The more she thought about it, the stronger the pull became to go for a little visit – anything to distract herself from thoughts of Scott.

She checked in on Miss Powell, who was snoozing peacefully in the front room, then made her way up the stairs to the attic.

Everything was exactly as she had left it. The key for the gilded mirror sat on the shelf beside it, tucked under a book. She slid the key into the lock and turned it.

Before stepping in, she paused to look at her reflection, straightening her hair and squaring her shoulders. Then she stepped inside. With the door closed behind her, she prepared herself for the transition.

Closing her eyes, she spun three times clockwise. This time, she was ready for the sensation of whirling through time and space, steadying herself against the cupboard walls so she wouldn't topple. When the strange vertigo eased, she opened her eyes and felt herself float through the door into the attic.

I'm getting good at this, she thought. The now familiar Victorian attic was scattered with old toys and clothes. She drifted down the stairs into the hall.

The house, one hundred years earlier, was alive with activity. Alison, the maid, was in the kitchen preparing tea, while Lily's father shouted for his wife from the living room. Lily's mother sighed but turned her attention to her daughter as she emerged from her bedroom.

Lily was dressed to go out – coat, boots, and hat in place.

'I really don't think you should bring that strange woman to this house,'

CHAPTER 28

her mother said. 'Your father is very upset today, and what can some gypsy woman possibly do but cause him more stress? Lily, you have the strangest ideas.'

Lily picked up a set of keys. 'Don't be ridiculous and so judgmental, Mother. I've heard remarkable stories about this lady and how she's helped other men suffering since they returned from the war. I've also heard talk at the asylum about the medicinal powers of certain plants - how powerful they can be - but their hands are tied, forced to use man-made drugs. Trust me on this. I only mean good for Father, and you know that.'

Her mother sighed. Though her daughter was stubborn and strong-minded, she knew her heart was in the right place. If Lily believed this woman could help, then she truly believed it.

'Go on, then, if you must. But please be careful in that new motor car - it goes so fast.' With that, she retreated into the living room.

Ella floated towards Lily, absorbing her energy. Today, she wanted to see Edinburgh through Lily's eyes. The sensation was immediate - she was a passenger in Lily's body. It felt both thrilling and strange, like wearing someone else's skin.

Lily stepped out the front door and into the garage, flinging open the doors to reveal a beautiful red car. A badge on the back read *Flying Fifteen* by Argyle Motors. She climbed in, started the engine, and pulled out onto the road, turning right towards Morningside.

Ella wondered about the gypsy woman mentioned earlier, but soon forgot as the streets pulled her into their spell. The buildings around her stood cleaner, sharper, unmarked by decades of soot and traffic fumes. Shopfronts brimmed with feathered hats, velvet gloves, and polished boots, their windows edged with hand-painted signs boasting *Finest Goods* and *Tailor-Made Suits*.

The people captivated her: women in neat 1920s hats and calf-length dresses, heels tapping on the cobbles, some pushing enormous prams. Men in suits and bowler hats exchanged nods as they passed. The air carried the rumble of distant trains, the groan of wooden buses, and the creak of horse-drawn carts. A mingled scent of coal smoke and fresh bread floated on the breeze.

Lily drove on, passing the green sweep of the Meadows. Children darted between trees, couples strolled arm in arm, and nannies wheeled prams along shaded paths.

On the far side of the park, the scenery shifted - tenements rose in tight rows, laundry lines stretched from window to window, and the streets bustled with trams, carts, and shouting children. This was the working-class south side. Clothes on many of the children were little more than rags, but the place was alive with noise and neighbourly banter.

The car turned onto a street Ella recognised as the site of one of her favourite pubs - The Pear Tree. But here, in this time, it was still a small farm with an orchard, and a yard of clucking hens and snorting pigs.

Lily parked further up the road. Instantly, a dozen children swarmed the car, touching it, asking rapid-fire questions: 'How come a woman can drive a car?' 'How does it work?'' 'I'll watch it for you, Missus, for sixpence!'

Smiling, Lily handed out a few pennies. 'All right, boys - you look after my car, and there'll be sweets when I return.' They stood tall, proud to be looking after such a polished car.

Lily pushed open a red door into a stairwell - the shared entrance to a tenement. The air was musty, the stone steps worn smooth. Cooking smells spilled from the doors she passed.

On one landing, she almost collided with an old man stepping out. The stench of sewage hit her - the shared stair toilet. He looked startled to see such a well-dressed young woman in his stair. She managed a quick hello before moving on.

At the second landing, she rapped on a black door with a gleaming brass knocker. Rose opened it. They could not have looked more different: Lily's dark bob against Rose's coppery-red bun, green eyes, pale skin, and freckles scattered over her nose.

'Hello, Miss Fraser,' said Rose. 'I'm ready.' She picked up a basket laden with herbs - some dried, some fresh - and small brown bottles.

They descended the stairs, their footsteps echoing. Outside, the red car gleamed like a jewel against the soot-stained backdrop. The boys, true to their word, had stood guard. Lily rewarded them with a paper bag of boiled

CHAPTER 28

sweets before they scattered, shouting and laughing.

Rose hesitated before climbing in, straightening her shawl under the watchful eyes of her neighbours. She had never ridden in a car before. The engine roared to life, making her grip the seat.

They didn't speak on the journey – the noise made it impossible – but both women were thinking about the same thing: the man they hoped to help.

In the 1920s, the public knew nothing of what we now call shell shock. The government denied its existence, but these two women had seen its effects firsthand.

When they arrived, Lily parked in the garage and led Rose into the house. She introduced her to her mother before guiding her to the living room. Her father sat in a chair, staring into space.

'Father, this is Rose. She's here to listen to you and see if she can help.' Lily's voice softened as she looked at him. He gave no sign he had even heard her.

Rose glanced at Lily. 'I'd like a little time alone with your father, if that's all right.'

Chapter 29

Meanwhile, while Ella was stepping through the golden mirror into another time, Scott arrived at Miss Powell's house, half-hoping to catch sight of her in the garden.

But the part of the garden where she usually pottered was empty. When he asked Miss Powell if she'd seen her, she shook her head. 'She can't be far, Scott - we had a cup of tea together not long ago.' He tried not to feel disappointed. It wasn't as if he had the right to expect her to be there - but he'd been looking forward to chatting a bit. Instead, he headed to his van for his tools, only to spot Janey strutting down the hill. She came right up to him.

'Ooh, this is a nice surprise,' she said, her gaze sliding deliberately over him.

Scott had seen her around and knew she was Ella's sister. He recognised the look in her eyes and felt a bit uneasy. He didn't want a scene.

Janey remembered Ella brushing off any interest in Scott. Well, if her sister wasn't interested, Janey decided, she was free to make her move.

She'd dressed with care - leggings, a clingy cropped top, her favourite Dr. Martens - a mix of sexy and edgy that she knew worked for her.

'Where's Ella then?' she asked, though her focus never left him. 'I've no idea,' he said. 'Miss Powell doesn't know either. Maybe she's gone for a walk.' Scott got ready to walk away, but Janey had other ideas. 'Aw, that's a shame, it's just me and you then,' Janey said in a voice that definitely didn't sound like she thought it was a shame. She stepped into his space and brushed her chest against him.

Scott stiffened. He couldn't help noticing her body - he was a man, after

CHAPTER 29

all – but his mind, he wasn't interested in Janey. This was Ella's sister, and he could tell she was in trouble, and he didn't want to have anything to do with her.

Janey, misreading him, pressed closer. 'Maybe we can have some fun in the meantime, Scott,' she murmured.

He stepped back. 'Sorry – but I'm not interested.'

Ignoring the flare of annoyance in her eyes, he picked up his tools and stepped away. Janey was used to men falling for her, and when she realised she had misread Scott, she got mad at him for not wanting her and her cheeks flushed with embarrassment at the situation.

She could have walked away at that point, but instead, her voice rose.

'Who the hell do you think you are? Walking away from me? I've seen the way you've looked at me. Now I make a move and you walk away?'

Scott hated scenes. He just wanted to get on with his work and get away from this situation. Being a good-looking guy sometimes brought trouble that he could do without. He knew he needed to walk away from this scene before it got messy.

What neither of them knew was that Miss Powell was pottering in the garden and had heard every word. *That girl is just making trouble for herself,* she thought.

As Janey ranted, Scott thought of how different the two sisters were – Ella's easy smile, and the way she looked great every day without even trying – and wondered where she'd gone.

Because this morning, of all mornings, he'd much rather have found her there instead of her sister.

Chapter 30

Ella wasn't aware of any of this, as she was with her new friends – in the same house, but in a different time.

She watched Rose walk into the front drawing room to meet with Lily's father. She didn't feel it was right to watch Rose work with Mr Fraser, and besides, Ella's energy was still attached to Lily. So, when Lily went into the other sitting room, where her mother was waiting for Rose to finish, Ella went too.

She looked around the room and decided they might be sitting here for a while.

It felt like a good time to get back to her own time and place. She pulled her energy away from Lily and spun around, free to go where she wanted. Ella could have sworn Lily gave a little shudder as she left, but she couldn't be sure.

Ella felt the cold creep in as she detached herself from Lily. Part of her was tempted to go back and attach herself again. When she was with Lily, she felt warm, safe, and protected. She didn't have to make decisions about what to do, say, or think – and she was enjoying that. She liked being part of a strong woman, carried along by her focused thinking and decisive actions. It was an escape from her own life – from her inability to feel confident, to speak her mind, or to take positive action sometimes.

She floated back towards Lily, ready to wrap her energy around her again. Then a thought struck – *What day is it? Is Scott going to the house today?*

She stopped just short of Lily and reminded herself of her own life: her cosy bedroom, and the warm feeling she got when she saw Scott.

CHAPTER 30

What am I doing?

It would be too easy to stay there, wrapped up in these people's lives. But she knew it was time to get back to her own.

She floated away from Lily, giving her a silent goodbye as she left the living room, drifted into the hall, and pushed her energy through the attic door. She found the golden mirror and stepped into the dark space behind it.

She set her intention to return to her own time and place. When the world stopped whirling around her, she pushed open the door and stepped into the familiar attic of her home.

Turning to the mirror, she caught sight of her reflection – solid, real, back where she belonged.

She hurried down the attic stairs, craving her sofa and the chance to process all she had seen – especially the old streets of Edinburgh. She was blown away by the experience and couldn't help wondering how Rose was getting on with Lily's father.

But another thought was already tugging at her... she really wanted to see Scott – after just a little rest between worlds.

Chapter 31

As she walked toward her bedroom, Janey came storming in from the garden. Her cheeks were flushed and her eyes glittered with anger. Drama was the last thing Ella had hoped for - what was Janey doing here anyway? Watching her little sister stomp toward her, Ella thought, *I'm not sure I'm in the mood for one of her dramas.* 'That Scott is horrible!' shouted Janey, running up to her sister. 'I have no idea why Miss Powell keeps him about. She mustn't know what he's really like. You were right to say he was a creep.'

Ella froze - the leap from Lily's peaceful calm to Janey's hurricane energy was jarring. 'Wait a minute, Janey - what are you talking about? Anyway, I never, ever said Scott was a creep. All I've said is that he wouldn't be interested in a girl like me. I think Scott is a nice guy, and to be honest, I think he's pretty damn hot - but I haven't got around to telling him yet. What's your problem with him?'

'Are you serious?' said Janey. 'I thought you didn't even like him. You weren't bothered about him not coming to the pub the other night.'

'Well, what did you want me to do? Cry into my drink because he never showed up? Hardly my style, is it?' Ella shot back. 'Maybe you should have asked me how I felt if you were that interested. Anyway, why are you here calling him names, Janey? Honestly, I can do without this right now.'

But Janey ploughed on as if she hadn't heard. 'Scott just came on heavily to me. He pressed up hard against me and told me he wanted me, and when I said I wasn't interested, he pushed me against the wall and tried to touch me.' Her voice dropped to a low, deliberate tone, as if she was trying to give more weight to her words that she knew were not true. Janey paused, watching

CHAPTER 31

Ella's face, almost convincing herself this was what had happened. *Now that she'd stuck the knife in Scott, why not twist it?* It would be easier if he just disappeared from the picture.

'I'm telling you, Ella, you're better off without him. Anyway, Rab says he's a drug addict, used to be homeless - and get this - he's been in prison too. Bet he hasn't told you that.' Ella blinked, trying to take it in. Scott coming on to Janey and treating her badly? That didn't sound like him at all.

In the past, she'd have stepped back, avoided the drama. But now she found herself thinking, h*ow would Lily deal with this?* Lily wouldn't let an injustice slide - and neither would she.

'I'm not understanding this at all, Janey. This doesn't sound like the Scott I know.'

Before, she wouldn't have thought about questioning her sister. Now she pushed past that fear. 'Janey, this is a serious accusation. I think it's only fair we hear Scott's side before we involve Miss Powell. Let's go see him now.'

Janey hadn't expected that. She'd counted on Ella's old habit of wanting a quiet life and no confrontations. This was new territory.

From the living room, Miss Powell sat quietly, listening through the open window. She hadn't meant to overhear, but she'd already caught Janey's earlier exchange with Scott in the garden. She'd wait to see how Ella handled it - a good test of her character. Ella brushed past Janey and headed out. 'Where are you going?' demanded Janey.

'To find Scott. What you told me is serious - I need to hear his side.'

In the garden, Scott was halfway up his ladder. He looked down, wary, having heard Janey's loud voice from inside the house. Ella didn't look angry, and figured that had to be a good thing.

She took a deep breath. 'Janey says you came on to her, and when she said no, you pushed her against the wall. Is that what happened, Scott?'

Scott stared, stunned. 'Ella, that is not the type of guy I am.' He glanced between the sisters. 'I think Janey's got it all a bit mixed up.' He looked straight at Janey, hoping she could see that he just wanted to resolve the horrible situation caused by her lies. 'She thought I fancied her, came in close, and I told her I wasn't interested and stepped away. As she walked away, she kinda bumped into the ladder, and it startled her, and she got a bit upset and ran off.'

Janey hesitated – even she could see Scott was giving her a way out. 'Aye... he's right. I got embarrassed, worked myself up, and it all came out wrong when I told you.'

Ella fixed her with a steady look. 'Janey, you can't go around making up stories like that. One day it could land you in real trouble.' Janey mumbled something that might have been an apology.

'And another thing,' Ella added. 'You brought up Scott's past even though it has nothing to do with you or me. Miss Powell knows him from his volunteering days, and I know she trusts him, and the truth is, I trust Scott too.'

She glanced at him, smiling. 'It's better to talk things through instead of letting misunderstandings fester. Maybe we can have that cup of tea together later?' She knew how upsetting this must have been for him, and she knew her fiery sister's temper and liking for drama as well.

Scott smiled in relief. 'That sounds great.' He climbed back up the ladder happy to get on with his day.

Chapter 32

Ella looked at Janey in despair. Sometimes her sister seemed so different from her, so far removed from how she saw the world, that it was difficult to even like her - let alone love her. Over the years, Janey's dramas had caused so many problems that Ella was tired of helping her out of them. Even though Janey was the older one, it felt like Ella had spent her life looking after her.

She took a long, hard look at her sister and softened when she saw how upset Janey looked. Her body language had shifted from anger and defensiveness to shame and embarrassment. Ella felt she was getting the message through and began to feel a bit sorry for her.

Janey looked up with tears in her eyes. 'Aye, I got a bit out of hand, I have to admit. I guess I'm not used to people saying no, and I got angry with him and then myself.' She paused. 'You do know I don't care about his past. I know I'm no angel, and I know Rab isn't either. I wouldn't want people shouting about his past. I get it - I was just saying all that to get a reaction from you.'

Janey looked searchingly at her sister, wanting her approval - a very new emotion for her. 'I was angry and hitting out. That was shitty of me, and I can see that now.'

She looked at Ella with a new admiration. 'When did you get all grown up?' She asked. Ella took it in. She had handled that pretty well, she thought. The old her would have let this stew for days, weeks, even months - and it would have slowly eaten away at any trust she had in Scott. Instead, it was all sorted in minutes. Ella was pretty sure she had her friend Lily, from a hundred years ago, to thank for her newfound confidence.

Ella smiled. 'I guess we all have to grow up sometimes.'

Janey shrugged, smiled back, and asked, 'Cup of tea?' She was tempted just to leave – she wasn't one for talking about feelings, especially when things hadn't gone her way – but she could feel something had shifted in Ella. She was trying to understand her and not be angry. It was the right thing to do to smooth things over. With a bit of a shock, Janey realised the last thing she wanted was to fall out with her only sister.

She helped Ella make the tea, and they went into the front room, where Miss Powell sat quietly in her rocking chair. 'Ah, a lovely cup of tea for us,' she said, putting her book down. 'Everything is okay now.' Ella realised this wasn't a question but a statement. Miss Powell clearly knew something had happened that afternoon and Ella wondered how much she had overheard.

'Everything is good, isn't it, Janey?' Ella passed her a cup and smiled. 'Aye, everything's okay, thanks.'

Miss Powell was pleased. All was sorted without her needing to interfere. Her new student was proving she wasn't afraid of the truth and valued communication – so important in the work of a healer. She was glad Ella had trusted her intuition and asked the right questions.

Janey looked over at Ella. It was unsettling that Ella had the nerve to challenge her, but she was also glad. Things could have quickly got out of control if Miss Powell had been told – or worse, if the police had been called. How would she explain that to her possessive, often angry boyfriend?

She thought back to when they were kids. Even then, they were so different. Janey had been more concerned with her looks, the latest fashions, and having material things. Ella saw fairies at the bottom of the garden, made up stories about them, and had invisible friends.

Ella never liked to challenge anyone and often moulded herself to fit into other people's lives and plans. She preferred the quiet life and rarely complained – unlike Janey.

As Janey sat in the peaceful living room, her mind wandered further back. The sisters had lost their parents in a terrible accident when Janey was five and Ella was three. They grew up in a variety of children's and foster homes before a lovely couple adopted them. In time, the girls came to love them just as deeply as they were loved.

CHAPTER 32

Sadly, their adopted dad died when they were still young, but Nancy kept the family together. The girls stayed close to her, visiting and calling often.

Janey remembered the foster homes before Nancy. If she wasn't happy or felt restricted, she lashed out at everyone - carers, social workers, and teachers. Everybody knew when Janey wasn't happy.

Ella was different. She adapted to whatever circumstances she found herself in, somehow finding peace wherever she was. Perhaps it was because she lived in her pretend world of invisible friends, fairies, and elves at the bottom of every garden.

When Janey turned thirteen, she blossomed into a lovely young girl, and men began to pay unwanted attention. Some older men saw her vulnerability and need for attention and took advantage. Janey became a rebellious teenager, often finding herself in tricky situations.

She thought it was her fault when bad things happened. If only she had told someone, it might have stopped. Her adopted mum and teachers knew nothing about the men who touched her or forced her into sexual acts.

Janey kept it secret, feeling ashamed and somehow responsible. At thirteen, she dealt with the pain by masking it with drink and drugs. She cut her arms and legs, watching the blood flow as if the pain was leaving her body.

As she grew, she moved from one toxic, manipulative relationship to another, unable to see they were wrong. She thought she deserved to be treated that way.

All these thoughts flowed through her now, sitting with Ella and Miss Powell. *What they didn't realise,* Janey thought, was that her coming on to Scott was her way of saying she thought he was a nice guy.

Janey didn't know how to just have a male friend. She shook her head to clear it - this was all getting a bit too deep.

She looked up from her tea to find Miss Powell watching her. Miss Powell smiled. 'You are welcome here, Janey. If you ever want to pop round for tea and a chat - or maybe one day I can do a reading for you.'

Janey looked over at the purple cloth where Miss Powell kept her beautiful tarot cards - cards she knew well from Ella's descriptions. She could tell Miss Powell knew what had gone on and was reaching out as a friend.

'Aye, thanks,' said Janey. 'I might do that one day.' She felt shy and, for once, was lost for words. 'I think it's time for me to go home now.'

She picked up her bag and coat, gave Ella a hug – unusual for her – said goodbye to Miss Powell, and left.

Chapter 33

Ella thought about everything she had experienced that day and how it had turned out. She had found it difficult to challenge Janey about her version of what had happened with Scott, but she was happy she had listened to her instincts and that the situation had been cleared up.

Ella was enjoying her newfound confidence, feeling it grow more each day. She was sure it had a lot to do with what she was experiencing on her journeys to the past. She kept thinking about the golden mirror, the magical journeys she had taken, and the characters she met a hundred years ago.

She realised she was daydreaming again, then looked across the room at Miss Powell and met her gaze. It brought her back into the present moment.

'Expect you heard some of what went on today,' said Ella to Miss Powell.

'Aye, lass. As you get older, you sometimes hear more than you want to, and sometimes you hear nothing at all. Your judgement of Scott was excellent, I'm glad to say.'

'Well, I knew you met him at a voluntary organisation, and you told me he used to be homeless and lived in a hostel. People who become homeless always have a story to tell. Who am I to judge what they've been through? I know you trust him, and that's good enough for me.'

'That is good. Too often, people jump to conclusions or make judgments based on where someone grew up or their appearance. I grew up with my fair share of people judging me and my family.' Miss Powell looked into the distance, as if seeing her past in front of her.

'I didn't know that,' said Ella. Miss Powell sat still for a moment, her fingers tracing the rim of her teacup. She hadn't spoken about this in years -

not because she was ashamed, but because it was easier not to talk about it. But something about Ella, with her quiet curiosity and open heart, made her think it was the right time to share.

'I don't talk about this often,' she said, a faint smile on her lips. 'But I think you'll find it interesting.' She let out a slow breath and met Ella's gaze.

'Truth is, lass, when your mother is full-blooded Romany and your father isn't, as their child, you don't belong to one side or the other. My mother was a healer and reader, and most people who met her loved her. But there was always someone who disliked her or was suspicious – just because of her bloodline.'

'Wow,' said Ella, thinking that made so much sense. 'So your bloodline is Gypsy? That is fascinating! Was it your mother who taught you about herbs and reading cards and tea leaves?'

Miss Powell laughed at Ella's description. 'Aye, she did that, lass. I tagged along on her coattails as soon as I could walk, learning all that she knew along the way. I didn't learn as much as I could have – not as much as my mother, that's for sure. This is why I want to share with you what I know about medicinal herbs. I have a feeling there is something special about you. If you nurture it, you can bring out the healer in you.'

Ella sat there, stunned. Her, a healer? The thought had never crossed her mind. Mind you, when she was a child, she had wanted to be a nurse or look after people in some way when she grew up. But that dream had faded over the years. Maybe it was time to revisit it.

'I haven't thought of myself as a healer, but I would love to learn more about the herbs in the garden and what they can do. I was looking there yesterday and got rid of a few of the weeds,' said Ella. 'I may do a bit more of that today.' She was also thinking it would be a great way to ground herself and reflect on what Miss Powell had said.

'You do that, lass,' said Miss Powell with a knowing nod. 'I suggest you take cuttings of the herbs you recognise, put them into your basket, and tomorrow, start learning about their healing powers.'

'Sounds great,' Ella said, already eager to get her hands in the earth. With that, she wandered off into the garden, enjoying the quiet pleasure

CHAPTER 33

of pottering among the plants.

In the garden, a thought began to take shape. The stories Miss Powell shared about her childhood, the glimpses Ella caught of Rose's life when she slipped through time – there was something similar in them, as if a thread was connecting the past and present. Could there be more to it? The idea settled in her mind, lingering like an unsolved riddle.

She thought back to the last time she had travelled back in time and was intrigued to know what had happened when Rose went to meet Lily's father.

She looked at her watch and worked out that she still had an hour or two before meeting Scott for lunch. It often felt like she was away for hours when she travelled back in time, but in reality, only minutes or an hour passed in her own world.

Feeling a slight tingle of excitement in her stomach, she made up her mind. She had enough time to go through the golden mirror and see what was happening.

Ella made her way up the stairs to the attic and stepped through the golden mirror. She spun around three times and pushed her way out again. Looking around, she recognised the ancient trunks and toys. She had stepped back in time again.

She floated down the stairs, excited by what she might see and who she might meet.

The old house was quiet. There was no bustling noise from the kitchen and no sign of Lily. Ella floated through to the drawing room and saw Lily's mother and father. Lily's father was deep in concentration, a drawing pad on his lap. Her mother had a slight frown and looked lost in thought.

'Perhaps we should have gone to the recital at the asylum tonight,' she said. 'Lily was very keen for us to go, to see the progress and the talents of some of her patients. It might have been nice to go.'

Her husband shrugged gruffly, hardly looking up from his drawing pad.

'I wasn't very kind to Lily about her idea of allowing that woman, Rose, to come up here to see you, but' – she gave him a little smile – 'I'm very glad we did, dear.' She looked at her husband fondly. 'You do seem better since Rose's visit, and it's so nice to see you drawing again. I haven't seen you do that since before the war.'

Her husband stopped what he was doing, gave a small smile to his wife, then went back to his drawing.

Ella could smell the distinct aroma of roses in the room. She saw a small, brown glass bottle labelled *Rose Petal Oil*.

Mr Fraser was sipping what looked and smelled like herbal tea. She was sure these were recent additions from Rose.

Curious to understand more, she attached her energy to Mrs Fraser, tuning into her thoughts.

Mrs Fraser looked at her husband with relief. If she had mentioned the war to him just a while ago, he would have roared at her. But since Rose's visit, he seemed calmer and more able to focus on the hobbies he once loved.

Rose had given Mrs Fraser an oil tincture made from beautiful Scottish red roses, created by infusing the petals in oil. She had encouraged her to dab a little onto her husband's pillow at night and around the cushions of the chair where he sat most of the day. When he took a bath, she suggested adding rose water, explaining that rose petals could calm and uplift the emotions and had a mild sedative effect. Rose had also left a mixture of herbs with similar properties for Mr Fraser to drink as tea, sweetened with a bit of honey.

At first, Mr Fraser grumbled about the herbal tea, but he quietly drank it when his wife or Lily placed it beside him.

After a couple of weeks, his spirits seemed to lift, and his nightmares and night sweats became less frequent.

For the first time in a long time, Mr Fraser complained of being bored and wanted something to do.

Lily was quick to respond to her father's need for activity and would bring him books, his old drawing pad, and his collection of pencils.

Mrs Fraser was delighted to see glimpses of the man he had been before the war.

Chapter 34

Ella could see that Rose's visit had made a difference to Lily's father. She moved her energy away from Mrs Fraser as she felt as if she was intruding on their moment.

She slipped away from the front drawing-room, leaving Mr and Mrs Fraser to enjoy their evening together.

Ella realised that although it had been morning when she stepped through the Golden Mirror, when she stepped out into the past, evening had already settled in.

When Mrs Fraser mentioned that Lily was at the asylum recital, Ella knew exactly where she wanted to be too. She had heard about the Grand Hall in the asylum and longed to see it herself and be there for the recital. With a quick calculation, she figured she had just enough time to experience it and still make it back in time to meet Scott for lunch.

Ella gathered her energy and got ready to move out of the house and up the hill.

Ella wasn't used to being outside on her own - she was usually attached to Lily, so she experimented with what she could do and sent her energy high into the sky. She looked down at the houses below; they seemed so small. This was such a good feeling that she was tempted to keep flying.

Looking down below, she could see the many buildings that made up the asylum. She decided to stick to her plan and took energy down to the asylum to look for Lily.

There were many cars in the long driveway, some with drivers in black uniforms and peaked caps, leaning against shiny cars and smoking, chatting to each other. The driveway was lit up with gas lights, as was the main entrance to the asylum. It all looked very magical.

Ella floated up to the main entrance, through the grand doorway, and up the sweeping staircase.

In the distance, she heard the notes of a piano drifting through the corridors, drawing her toward the Grand Hall. As she floated inside, her breath caught in her throat.

The room was magnificent - vast walls adorned with huge oil paintings and stately portraits, their watchful eyes seeming to follow her every move. A grand fireplace dominated one side, flames flickering and casting golden light across the polished wooden floor. Above, chandeliers hung from the soaring ceiling, their crystals catching the glow of gas lamps dotted around the hall, bathing the space in warm, amber light. Mounted moose and bear heads loomed from the walls, their solemn expressions frozen in time, overseeing the gathered guests below.

The air was a blend of aged wood, wax polish, and the faintest trace of smoke from the fire. She paused at the doorway, hardly able to believe she was witnessing this moment in history.

At the front was a grand piano, played by a man in a suit, his fingers gliding over the keys in a tune from a time gone by that Ella recognised.

The audience was a mix of elegantly dressed ladies and gentlemen, their clothes reflecting their status in life. Among them were many doctors and nurses still in their crisp uniforms, a reminder that despite the grandeur of the room, it was a hospital.

At the back of the Hall, another group of onlookers stood apart, some wrapped in worn dressing gowns, others in simple day clothes - setting them apart from the privileged guests. Their presence carried a quiet contrast, and Ella quickly understood these were the patients. In total, at least seventy-five people filled the room, their murmured conversations blending with the soft strains of the piano, creating an atmosphere of anticipation and quiet excitement.

Ella floated about, looking for Lily. She brought herself down to the level of the audience and, as she floated about, she had a feeling that she was being

CHAPTER 34

watched.

She spun her energy around to find out where this feeling was coming from. She was almost at the back of the Grand Hall where the patients were standing. There was a man of about fifty years of age, staring straight at her. Ella flew over to him. 'Can you see me?' asked Ella.

'Shh,' said the patient, 'we've waited all month for this recital, don't you know? Please get out of my way.' And the patient's focus went back to the piano as Ella floated away, wondering how on earth the patient could see her. It made her excited and scared at the same time. She remembered reading somewhere that sometimes people with schizophrenia and other similar illnesses could see things that others couldn't.

It was almost as if they lived in a different realm than everyone else. Ella quickly floated her energy away from the man and continued looking around. She was enjoying seeing the Great Hall being used to its fullest and finest capacity. She couldn't see Lily yet, but didn't mind so much. She couldn't resist; she wanted to explore the hospital in its full working glory.

She floated out of the Hall and up the stairs into the main body of the hospital. It was early evening, and all was quiet. The nurses were easily identifiable in their calf-length, slender white uniforms. They wore white stockings and black shoes with soft heels, so they made little noise as they walked. They wore starched caps with short veils hanging down the back of their hair. Very stylish, very 1920s, thought Ella.

The patients not at the recital were already locked into their wards or private suites by this time. She floated through many long corridors, some parts of the Hall so wide that they looked like living rooms sometimes.

Ella drifted effortlessly through the many locked doors, finding herself in what she first thought must be a residential part of the hospital for the staff, but then thought it was a bit too luxurious to be for staff, and it had a locked door. She floated back through the closed door and saw what she had missed the first time around, and it confirmed that this was indeed a ward. She guessed it must be for the wealthier patients. This time, she saw the faded lettering above the entrance: Ward 10. Instead of a stark, institutional feel, it was designed more like a private home, almost separate from the main asylum. Private locked bedrooms lined the corridor, while a communal living area, games room, bathrooms, showers, and even a kitchen created a sense of domesticity. Despite the locked doors, it didn't carry the heavy atmosphere of confinement – instead, it felt like a place meant to offer care and healing.

In complete contrast to this area, she floated through many cold and sterile wards with up to twenty beds in them, with a nursing station in the centre of the room. The ward carried a heavy, lived-in scent – a mixture of disinfectant, lingering meal odours, and the unmistakable smell of too many bodies in one place. The air felt thick and stale in places, as if it had absorbed the routines and restless nights.

Beyond this, the hospital had endless corridors and stairs that were lit up by gas lanterns, giving a slightly eerie feel to them. Up ahead, Ella could see a male doctor in a white coat. As she got closer, Ella realised that she recognised him.

It was Dr Ramsey, the doctor that Lily did not like at all. Ella could see he was standing uncomfortably close to a nurse. She saw him put his hand on the nurse's backside and squeeze it. The nurse pretended it didn't happen and sidestepped away from the doctor to put some distance between them.

Ella floated over to watch them from the front. The nurse's face distorted with a mixture of fear and hatred. Dr Ramsey appeared to be unaware of the effects his actions had on the nurse.

'Ah yes, our patient, Mr Blyth, I heard he refused to take his pills this evening,' said Dr Ramsey.

'Yes,' said the nurse, 'but he is doing so well. He was helping in the garden today, digging, weeding, making tea for the others and working well as part of the gardening team. He was happy and relaxed today. The last couple of nights, he has slept right through without his pills. Dr Clouston thinks this is a good time to reduce his pill intake and says he is on the road to recovery.'

'Indeed,' snorted Dr Ramsey, 'well, I don't tolerate behaviour like that. Even something that appears to be a small thing is the start of rebellion and disobedience to my rules and I will not stand for it.'

Two orderlies walked by, and Dr Ramsey commandeered them. 'You two. I would like you to retrieve patient John Blyth from Ward 13 and escort him to

CHAPTER 34

room 24 on the 6th floor. Take him by force if he won't go along by himself. I will see you there in 5 minutes.'

'It will take longer than five minutes to get him there, Doctor,' said one orderly.

'It certainly will if you stand here talking about it. Use a straitjacket if you need to, but just get the job done,' grunted Dr Ramsey.

Horrified by these commands, the nurse said to the doctor, 'There's no need to put him in a solitary room, and certainly no need to use a straitjacket. Mr Smith is a compliant, calm and responsive patient. Putting him into a straitjacket and solitary confinement could send him back into a state of shell shock.'

Dr Ramsey looked down at the nurse and scornfully said, 'As you know, I am your superior in every way. Do not try to tell me how to do my job; get on with your own. How dare you question me?' He turned and strode down the corridor, knowing his word was the final one.

The nurse was close to tears at her lack of authority to help her patient.

Chapter 35

Dr Ramsey's abrupt and arrogant behaviour horrified Ella. She wondered how she could help. Keen as she was to go and try and find Lily, she was concerned about what this doctor was about to do. As Dr Ramsey walked up the stairs, she floated after him, following him through a warren of corridors and staircases.

He took an enormous bunch of keys out and continued to pass through several more rooms. Eventually, he slowed down as they entered yet another long white corridor - but this one was different. The air here felt colder, heavier, as if the walls themselves had soaked up the despair and screams of hundreds, if not thousands, of patients over the years.

There were many doors off the corridor, each with numbers outside and small windows she could see through. What she saw was every nightmare she had ever imagined about old asylums made real.

The rooms could only be described as cells. Each one had padded white walls and a single, blinding light in the centre of the ceiling. There was no bed, only a pot in the corner, which Ella guessed was a toilet.

Each cell held one person. Some patients were strapped into straitjackets, their arms bound tight; some sat on the floor, rocking endlessly; others banged their heads against the wall in a dull, repetitive thud.

The corridor rang with an unsettling mixture of sounds - raw screams, muttered pleas, and the hollow silence of those staring into nothing. A chemical tang of disinfectant mixed with stale air, sweat, and the faint metallic scent of blood.

Some were lying on the floor, looking lost and utterly alone.

CHAPTER 35

Ella jumped when she peered through the window of cell number 18. The patient suddenly lunged toward the glass, mouthing the word *help.*

'I promise, I will try,' she mouthed back, startled that he could see her. The realisation struck her – some people *could* see her energy. Maybe she could do something to help them in this world.

When Dr Ramsey arrived in the corridor, he was enraged to find cell 24 still empty. He glanced around, looking for someone to shout at, but there was no one in sight.

Ella wanted to act. She had yet to materialise energy in this world; until now, she had simply shifted herself between places. But now she felt compelled to intervene.

She floated in front of Dr Ramsey and blew with all her energy into his face. He turned away, but she thought she saw a wisp of his hair move. Did he feel it? He didn't seem to, so she tried again – gathering all the energy she could and sending another rush of air into his face.

This time, the wisp of hair definitely moved. 'Shut all the bloody windows in this corridor,' barked Dr Ramsey at an orderly passing by. 'They are all closed,' the orderly replied. 'Not possible – I just felt a breeze. Double-check now and stop wasting my time.'

Ella's excitement grew – he *had* felt her. What else could she do to rattle him? She drifted back, then hurled herself forward, flying straight through his body.

Dr Ramsey bent double, clutching his stomach. 'What the hell was that?' he muttered, scanning the corridor.

Ella scanned for her next move. A table with a large plant pot stood nearby. Focusing her energy, she rammed into it. The pot tipped, fell, and smashed in an explosion of soil, shards, and flowers across the floor.

'What the hell...' Dr Ramsey said again, now visibly unsettled.

She surged forward until she was right in his face and screamed, 'Leave John Blyth alone! Send him back to his room. LEAVE HIM ALONE!'

Dr Ramsey spun around, his eyes widening. And then – the voices of the patients. Doors rattled and banged as they chanted, 'Leave him alone! Leave him alone!'

The corridor door burst open, and a tall, broad-shouldered woman in a dark uniform strode in. Her presence filled the space; Ella instantly knew she must be the Matron.

'Matron,' Dr Ramsey stammered, suddenly off balance.

'I do not know what you have done, or why you think you can come into my wards and upset the patients,' she said coolly. Her uniform was immaculate, her cap perfectly starched - and her eyes sharp. 'You have upset my ward and my patients, and I will not tolerate it. What exactly are you doing here?'

'I'm waiting for orderlies to bring John Blyth from Ward 13 to room 24, and things... somehow... got a little out of hand.'

The Matron's lips pressed into a thin line as she took in the chaos. The patients were still hammering on doors, shouting for John to be left alone. Dr Ramsey was visibly rattled - something Ella had never seen before.

'You,' said the Matron, seizing the moment, 'have upset the patients and the peace of this ward. You already know I disagree with most of these people being up here, locked away and drugged to the eyeballs. I will not stand by and watch another good man be put into solitary confinement unnecessarily. I know John Blyth is doing well - and I will not have you interfering.'

The double doors swung open again. Two orderlies appeared, wheeling a distressed patient strapped down with thick leather cuffs.

'Ah,' said Dr Ramsey, ignoring the Matron, 'John Blyth, room twenty-four, is ready for you.'

'Your behaviour towards this patient is unacceptable,' the Matron said sharply. 'Dr Ramsey, I think we can agree that John Blyth will *not* be occupying room twenty-four today. Or would you like me to file a report detailing the broken vase, screaming patients, and you standing in an empty corridor looking like a fool?'

She didn't need to finish her threat. Dr Ramsey's jaw tightened.

'Yes, of course,' he said through gritted teeth. 'Please remove his restraints immediately, orderly. This man is no threat.'

'It was you who insisted we restrain him if he didn't want to come,' one orderly muttered.

'Yes, I did,' Ramsey admitted reluctantly. 'I can see there's no need now.

CHAPTER 35

Remove them immediately.'

The orderlies freed John Blyth and wheeled him calmly back through the double doors.

The Matron's eyes bored into Dr Ramsey. 'I do not tolerate nonsense on my wards - doctor or no doctor. You haven't explained what happened here. Perhaps you need to see a psychiatrist yourself. Tomorrow I will personally assess all these patients with Dr Clouston. I want to be sure they're here for their good, not just on your orders.' She turned and strode down the corridor. 'I suggest you get a brush and shovel and clean up the broken pot. I cannot spare staff for such work. You'll find what you need in that cupboard.'

Left alone, Dr Ramsey looked pale. Ella couldn't resist - she shot her energy through his head this time. He wobbled, steadied himself, and shook his head before opening the cupboard.

The evening had not gone his way.

Ella, on the other hand, felt triumphant. She had helped - even if he didn't know it. With a lightness in her energy, she drifted back down to the Grand Hall to look for Lily.

Chapter 36

Lily, meanwhile, was enjoying the recital in the Grand Hall. The talents of the patients delighted her and the other audience members. There was a selection of patients performing poems, songs, and piano recitals. At the moment, a group of four young men - all patients - were on stage, their fingers dancing across saxophones, a trumpet, and a battered old upright bass, filling the Hall with a bright, brassy burst of jazz.

Lily found it hard to imagine that any of these performers would need to stay in the Asylum for much longer.

She looked around the Hall, taking in the scene. Gas lamps glowed softly along the walls, their light catching the polished brass fittings and shimmering across the faces of the audience. A faint scent of wax polish and cigar smoke lingered in the air, blending with the woody warmth from the fireplace.

She was proud to be a volunteer here and felt very much a part of the Asylum - but she wanted to do more.

She knew that wanting to study medicine, even in some capacity, was almost unheard of for a well-brought-up young lady. All of her school friends were already married and having children - a far more acceptable path for a woman of her age and background. But Lily felt her calling was to help others.

She was aware of the good work being done at the Asylum under the original guidance of Dr Clouston. His philosophy of fresh air, work, and creative outlets still breathed through some corners of the institution.

However, she also knew there was a darker side - and that some doctors preferred patients quiet and subdued, dosing them unnecessarily with drugs.

CHAPTER 36

Some unfortunate souls, especially under the likes of Dr Ramsey, endured what were called somatic treatments - restraints, cold baths, and worse. The very thought made Lily's stomach tighten, the cheerful music momentarily fading in her ears.

She wondered how she could expose these cruelties and bring about change in how patients were treated. Her mind wandered to *The Morningside Mirror*, the monthly magazine compiled by patients, featuring accounts of life inside, as well as fictional stories and poems.

It also advertised activities open to the public. The chief writer had approached Lily not long ago to ask if she would write an article. She had declined politely, believing her role too insignificant compared to that of other volunteers and staff.

But now she saw the magazine in a new light - not just a pleasant diversion, but a voice that reached beyond the Asylum walls.

What if she could give readers an insight into the more barbaric treatments? Surely, if the public knew what went on, there would be outrage, perhaps even reform.

She knew *The Morningside Mirror* served as the Asylum's mouthpiece, helping attract donors and fundraisers, and that it focused on the positive. She doubted they would willingly print anything darker - but the thought stayed with her.

Lily pulled her attention back to the present, letting the lilting strains of the jazz number wash over her. The musicians grinned at one another between notes, the rhythm infectious. Around her, heads nodded in time and feet tapped to the music and for a moment, the weight of the Asylum's shadows lifted.

Chapter 37

Ella found her way back to the Grand Hall and floated above the audience, looking for Lily. When she saw her, she paused, admiring her from a distance. The soft glow from the chandeliers caught the sheen of Lily's blue silk dress, which draped elegantly at the waist, the pleated skirt swaying just below her knees. She wore a simple string of pearls, white stockings, and black shoes with a small square heel. Lily looked truly beautiful, and Ella could see she was very much enjoying the performance in front of her.

Ella was delighted to have seen Lily at the concert, but she also felt she had seen enough for the evening. It was time to return to her own time. She floated out into the hall, down the stairs, and into the Asylum grounds.

She floated back down the hill to Lily's house and through the front door. All was quiet. She drifted upstairs into the attic, eager to return home.

She still found it thrilling to move between two worlds, and she felt incredibly fortunate to have experienced so much. But there was something different about this visit – a heaviness to the air, an almost watchful presence.

Today, different people had seen her, and others had felt her presence. That brought a genuine sense of satisfaction – she had done something worthwhile. Helping others felt good, and she wanted to carry that intention into her own world. Learning about healing herbs – like Rose – might be her way forward.

As she stepped towards the golden mirror, she pushed her energy through the mirror into the dark space behind and focused her energy on returning. She pushed herself into the doorway – and froze. A cold dread crept through her. She was still in Lily's attic, a hundred years in the past.

Panic rose in her chest. What was going on? Why was she still there? She

CHAPTER 37

tried again, gathering her energy and pushing hard against the mirrored door. Nothing.

Her mind jumped to the thought of being trapped here forever, the mirror just a lifeless slab of glass. The attic, once a place of wonder, now seemed like a prison.

She thought of her life – her friends, her work, her home – and realised she had been too casual about time travel. She needed to approach the mirror with more focus and respect.

Closing her eyes, she focused on the magical space behind the mirror, visualising herself spinning through time and space until she landed back in her own world. She pushed her energy forward and slipped back into the sacred dark space.

Relieved but determined, she spun three times, feeling the familiar rush of movement. When she touched the door and felt her flesh and blood hand again, she almost laughed with relief. She stepped out into Miss Powell's attic.

Back in her own world, she vowed never to travel between times so casually again. The thought of being stuck was too terrifying. She took a deep breath and thanked the universe for bringing her back safely.

She was sure she hadn't been away long, but when she went downstairs, the house was quiet. It was after three in the afternoon. Time had flown.

In the living room, Miss Powell sat in her favourite chair, reading.

'Gosh, I'm sorry about lunch, Miss Powell – the time just disappeared,' said Ella.

'Don't worry, my dear. I had a cheese scone, and Scott made me a lovely cup of tea. If I'm not mistaken, he seemed to be looking for you,' Miss Powell replied.

'Me? Oh, I don't think so... Wait a minute.' Ella remembered. 'Was it only this morning that Janey was here, with all that nonsense about Scott?'

Miss Powell gave her a strange look.

Ella suddenly realised she had promised to have lunch with Scott. Dammit. She had only meant to be away for half an hour.

'We were going to look at some of the herbs in the garden and begin learning their medicinal properties today as well,' Miss Powell said, her tone tinged with disappointment.

Miss Powell wondered if she had chosen her student wisely. Learning about herbs took dedication, not just curiosity. But she decided to give Ella another chance.

'It's a lovely afternoon. Let's take a walk around the herb garden. You can point out the plants you know, and we'll take it from there.'

'I'd love to,' Ella said quickly, relieved she hadn't ruined her chance. Letting down two people in one day would have been too much.

She straightened her posture, thinking of Lily and how she would seize such an opportunity with both hands. The thought made her smile, a swell of gratitude warming her chest.

Together, they stepped into the garden.

Chapter 38

Ella settled down on her comfy sofa in her room after spending a fascinating afternoon with Miss Powell. Her elderly friend knew a thing or two about herbs, that's for sure! Ella had pointed out the ones she knew - mint, rosemary, and sage - and her wise friend Miss Powell had told her when to harvest them, what ailments they could be used for, and the many different ways they could be prepared, such as in oils, drinks like teas, or as tinctures.

Miss Powell had said that if there were enough wildflowers and plants around, a person could find all they needed to stay healthy within a mile of their home. Ella was fascinated by their power, and she could tell this was just a taste of Miss Powell's knowledge.

She was glad to have spent time with Miss Powell and not let her down.

Scott, on the other hand - she had not shown up for. She had been too late for him. She had been more concerned about what was happening a hundred years ago instead of paying attention to her real life. *I have to be more mindful and careful of my time,* she scolded herself, then smiled, because she also felt she was learning and changing by observing Lily's life. She was sure Lily's strength of character was inspiring her in real life, too.

Standing up to Janey, she felt, was just the tip of the iceberg. Ella could feel her self-confidence growing every day. She wondered what Lily would do with the opportunities she had today.

Ella turned her thoughts to Miss Powell. Her health and energy levels were amazing - great for anyone of any age, never mind a lady in her seventies or eighties! She didn't know Miss Powell's exact age, but whatever it was, she was strong, mobile, and as sharp as a button. Her skin was healthy and glowing, with a few lines around her eyes and mouth - the kind that come from a life well lived and full of smiles.

Miss Powell did not take any prescription drugs from her GP, and in fact, Ella couldn't remember the last time she had needed to visit the doctor.

Ella often saw Miss Powell coming out from the room at the front of the house, though she had never been invited inside. Usually, when she passed that door, she caught a whiff of essential oils and flowers. The scent was lovely, and it made her curious.

Miss Powell would often ask Ella to make her one of her herbal teas. There was a vast array of jars containing dried herbs - chamomile, peppermint, echinacea, ginger, sage, mint, and many more. Miss Powell would ask Ella to put different combinations into a pot and pour hot water over them. The fresh teas fascinated Ella, and she would often enjoy a cup with Miss Powell.

Miss Powell also had a variety of small brown bottles beside her, each with handwritten labels, from which she would take little sips throughout the day. Sometimes she disappeared into her study for hours on end, and the next thing Ella knew, Miss Powell would have restocked her herbs in the kitchen.

Ella remembered what their neighbour, Mrs Donaldson, had told her about the house - how it used to be so busy with people coming and going. Mrs Donaldson had encouraged her to speak to Miss Powell about it, but Ella hadn't yet. Perhaps now was a good opportunity.

Carrying in a cup of herbal tea, she asked, 'Can I have a cup of tea with you?' Miss Powell put her book down and said, 'Of course.'

'I enjoyed learning a little about your herb garden yesterday,' said Ella. 'Thank you for taking the time to explain more about the herbs I do know. They have amazing healing powers I didn't know about - there seems to be a lot to learn. Miss Powell looked at her thoughtfully. 'Aye lass, that there is. To learn about the magical uses of herbs and plants takes time and dedication. To learn what to look for, how to identify and use them, means a lot of reading, studying, and foraging. Are you ready and prepared to do that?'

Ella could see that Miss Powell was serious and felt that this was an important question - one that could potentially change the direction of her life. She felt the intensity of Miss Powell's gaze, saw the wisdom in her eyes, and felt ready to step into something new.

'Yes, I am,' replied Ella. 'I'm beginning to think that my path is to help others – and I need someone, in the present, to guide and mentor me.'

Miss Powell tilted her head at the phrase *in the present* but didn't comment. 'The first step is to have a look at my collection of books, herbs, and tinctures from over the years,' she said mysteriously.

Chapter 39

Miss Powell led her out of the sitting room and down the hall, stopping in front of the mysterious door at the front of the house. Ella felt a rush of anticipation at what might be behind it.

Miss Powell took a large key from her apron, unlocked the door, and pushed it open. 'Come in,' she said.

Ella stepped inside and could hardly believe her eyes. It felt as though she were stepping back in time again - but this time, she knew she was still in the present.

Miss Powell took a seat in the large winged leather chair by the fireplace, watching Ella's face as she took it all in.

The room could have been a film set - an old-fashioned apothecary, the kind you might see in a period drama. The scent of flowers, herbs, and magical oils filled her nostrils. It smelled divine.

Ella's gaze roamed the space. Long wooden shelves lined two walls, crammed with bottles and jars of every shape and size, each filled with dried plants, fragrant herbs, and coloured oils. Cabinets were scattered throughout, their many small drawers neatly labelled in careful handwriting.

In the centre stood a freestanding counter with a smooth marble top. Upon it sat an antique writing bureau, an old-fashioned weighing scale, a large pestle and mortar, wooden boxes, and a tall container filled with tiny glass tubes. A stack of large, leather-bound ledgers lay nearby, their worn covers hinting at years of careful record-keeping.

It was an extraordinary sight. Shelves overflowed with labelled bottles of essential oils, while a nearby bookcase was packed with volumes on herbs,

CHAPTER 39

plants, and natural remedies.

Ella stood in the middle of the room, letting the atmosphere wash over her. The air felt rich with ancient wisdom. She loved it instantly - and felt at home here, ready to learn.

'This room is incredible,' said Ella, looking at Miss Powell in wonder. 'I didn't know there was such an amazing collection of herbs, oils, and tinctures in here! It's like stepping back in time. It feels as if this has been here forever.'

Miss Powell chuckled. 'Not forever - but more than one lifetime of knowledge is here, that's for sure.'

Ella looked at her. Miss Powell's eyes were shining, and sitting in her chair, she looked twenty years younger. It was as though the joy she saw in Ella's face was reflected in her own.

Ella had a torrent of questions. She reached for jars and bottles that caught her eye, opening each one to inhale its scent before asking what it was, where it came from, and what magical or healing powers it held. Whatever her question, Miss Powell had an answer. Her knowledge was vast, and Ella found herself hanging on every word.

After a while, Miss Powell reached up to a high shelf and pulled down two books, setting them on the counter with a satisfying thud. 'That's enough questions and answers for today,' she said with a knowing smile. 'I think you've got plenty to think about - but I want you to take these two books to start your studies.'

Ella took the books. One, simply titled *Herbs*, was an ancient brown hardback. When she opened it, the thin, well-worn pages crackled softly, the edges smudged from years of use.

The other was more modern but still had a vintage feel - *The Modern Herbal Dispensary* by Thomas Easley - filled with pictures, notes, mixtures, and recipes.

Miss Powell gave her a brief guide to the books on the shelves. She suggested Ella start with the two in her hands and then find each herb or oil mentioned among the jars, opening them, smelling them, and getting a true sense of each one.

She also gave Ella permission to read the old ledgers and learn from them.

Ella perched on a high wooden stool by the counter, surrounded by books, herbs, and tinctures. Miss Powell unlocked the writing bureau, revealing an array of fountain pens, ink, pencils, and stacks of fine writing paper.

Inside was a brand new leather-bound ledger. Miss Powell placed it before her. 'For your notes,' she said, certain now that she had found a worthy student in Ella.

Chapter 40

At the other side of the city, Scott had picked up a fish supper on his way home and was looking forward to it. He pulled up outside his block of flats, the warm, salty smell making his mouth water.

As he climbed the stairs, his thoughts turned to Ella - not for the first time. These days, she was often on his mind. He couldn't quite work her out. Why did she keep disappearing on the days they'd arranged to have a cup of tea or lunch together? She didn't seem like the type to play games.

Still... sometimes she seemed so distracted, it was as if she were in a completely different world. *Women can be so complicated*, he thought. He realised he had missed seeing her the day before.

It was odd - she'd say they'd meet, then vanish, only to reappear later looking flushed and slightly confused. He had no idea what was going on with her.

The truth was, he liked her more than he wanted to admit. And he didn't like the feeling he got when she didn't follow through on her promises. But a lifetime of disappointments - from his mother and others - had taught him to pack away feelings of hurt or frustration into a mental box and ignore them.

Over the years, his heart had developed a thin layer of a shell, an invisible shield against getting hurt. He wasn't aware of it consciously - it was just how he'd learned to be.

The sharp buzz of the entry phone dragged him back into the moment. Scott answered, opened the door - and there stood his ex-girlfriend, Tracy.

She was small, petite, blonde... and looking hot tonight.

'Hey, Scott. Was passing by and saw your light on - thought I'd come by and say hi.' Scott looked at her, trying to work out what she was doing here... and how he felt about it. Their relationship had been built on sex, heavy drinking, and nights out clubbing. Tracy had always carried a handful of pills she'd try to tempt him with, but drugs had never been his thing. But very much her thing. Being around her highs sometimes was fun, but the crushing lows that followed were not.

If he were honest, it had been a shallow, exhausting relationship. When she'd stopped answering his texts and things had fizzled out, he'd been relieved.

Now she was here again - looking good and ready for fun - and for a fleeting moment, he thought about how easy it would be to fall into a night of drinking and sex.

But looking closer, he realised he wasn't attracted to her anymore. She would be nothing but a distraction - and a complicated one at that. *No*, he decided. *Definitely not worth the hassle.*

'Um... hi, Tracy.' He made up his mind on the spot. 'To be honest, I'm just getting ready to go out,' he said evenly. Then, with a touch more weight: 'Turns out I'm seeing someone else now.'

It wasn't true - more wishful thinking - but he knew he was burning his bridges. He also knew he wanted more from a relationship than they had ever shared.

'And next time you just *happen* to walk by,' he added, fixing her with a look, 'best keep walking. I've moved on.'

Her eyes narrowed. 'Eh? What do you mean, *keep on walking*? Sod you, Scott - don't worry! You won't see me again.'

Tracy spun on her heel and stomped down the stairs, not used to being told to go away. Her blonde hair flicked over her shoulder in a gesture that was supposed to look careless, but her angry steps and the slam of the stair door told a different story.

Scott leaned against the closed door, satisfied with his decision. That would have been messy. He picked up his takeaway, settled in front of the TV, and pressed play to carry on watching a film.

Chapter 41

The next few weeks flew by for Ella. She loved studying with Miss Powell and quickly discovered a natural gift for working with herbs and plants. She spent hours in the garden alongside her mentor, learning the ways of the plants.

By mid-June, with the Summer Solstice approaching, Miss Powell explained that around June 21st, the herbs would be at their most potent - a perfect time to harvest and dry them. 'The more you harvest certain bushes, the more they'll flourish,' she told her.

Ella soaked it all in. She asked question after question, and Miss Powell enjoyed answering every one. In fact, she realised she had forgotten just how much she knew until she began sharing it again.

Miss Powell showed Ella her favourite local spots for gathering wild herbs. Ella would return with a basket brimming with what some might call weeds, but which she was beginning to see as treasures - each with magical properties.

The humble dandelion, for example, had quickly become one of her favourites. Packed with vitamin C and powerful antioxidants, it could help protect against heart disease, cancer, and other illnesses. Rich in minerals and nutrients, dandelions were far from weeds - their roots could be used in medicine, and tea could be made from their stalks and golden flowers.

Ella now drank herbal tea daily and felt the benefits - her mind felt clearer, her energy higher. Her leather-bound ledger, a gift from Miss Powell, was filling fast with her notes. And with every page, she learned a little more about Miss Powell herself. The older woman had yet to tell her full life story, but glimpses slipped through in the stories she shared.

The apothecary - or 'the study,' as Ella now called it - felt like a piece of history waiting for its story to be told.

Summer was warm and bright, and Ella loved pottering in the garden. She was so engrossed in her studies that she pushed thoughts of Scott to the back of her mind. Since the day she'd failed to meet him for lunch, he had grown distant, chatting with Miss Powell but barely acknowledging Ella. She took the hint that he wasn't interested, and told herself she didn't mind. Still, when he came to work in the garden, she found herself watching him from a distance.

On one particularly fine day, she went out to gather herbs. The distant hum of a hedge trimmer told her Scott was there. *Of course*, she thought. *It's Wednesday.*

She was absorbed in her picking when a sudden clatter from the other side of the hedge made her jump. She heard the sound of metal hitting the ground, followed by a cry.

'What on earth - ? Scott!' she shouted. 'Are you okay?'

Ella ran to the bottom of the garden, slipped through the gate, and hurried up the street. Scott was sprawled on the pavement, the ladder tipped over, the trimmer by his side. A pool of blood was forming beneath his hand - or maybe his head; she couldn't tell.

She carefully moved the trimmer and saw a large dog disappearing around the corner. Scott was still.

'Scott, can you hear me?'

'Aye, don't shout so loud,' he groaned. 'I'm alright... I think. Just cut my hand. That bloody dog ran into my ladder and I lost my balance.'

'Shh. Let's have a look.'

By now, Miss Powell had heard the commotion and was watching from the garden gate as Ella helped Scott inside. His face was pale, and the tea towel Ella had wrapped around his hand was already soaking through with blood.

She steered him into the bathroom and told him to keep the pressure on the tea towel to stem the flow of blood. 'I'll be back in a minute,' she told him, then dashed to the hallway.

Almost colliding with Miss Powell, she blurted, 'Can I use your study? Scott cut his hand on the trimmer – it looks worse than it is, but – '

'Of course, lass. But mind – this is the moment to stay calm and think. What have you learned that could help him?'

'But you'll know exactly what to give him,' Ella said desperately.

'Aye, but I won't always be here. This is your chance to put your learning into practice. I'll be here if you need me.'

Ella bit back a retort, then realised Miss Powell was right. Stepping into the study, she drew a deep breath. The familiar scent of oils and herbs steadied her.

A small smile crept over her face – she knew what to do. She gathered a few jars and bottles, selected a small glass vial from the case with all the homoeopathic jars in it, and prepared a compress of herbs and olive oil.

Returning to the bathroom, she found Scott leaning against the wall and looking pale. 'Can I go sit down for a bit?' he asked.

'Alright,' she said, removing the tea towel and inspecting the wound. She swapped out the tea towel and wrapped the herbal compress snugly around his hand, securing it with a safety pin. Then she cooled a towel under the tap, wrung it out, and patted his forehead. 'Come and sit down.'

He followed her into the living room, grateful – and a little pale at the sight of his own blood. She handed him two tiny white pills. 'They're homoeopathic – Arnica, for shock and bruising. Let them melt under your tongue.'

Ella found Miss Powell in her study again. 'Write down everything you used,' she instructed.

Ella quickly filled a page in her ledger, then handed it over. Miss Powell scanned it, nodded. 'Excellent choices. I couldn't have chosen better myself.'

They returned to find Scott sleeping on the sofa. 'Normal after shock,' Miss Powell said.

Ella studied him quietly – the shape of his nose, his cheekbones, the fall of blond hair over his eyes. She wondered what it might feel like to brush it back, to kiss him.

Scott stirred, caught her looking, and gave her a cheeky wink. 'Thanks, matey, for looking after me.

Chapter 42

Over the next few days, Ella felt more connected to herself. Having treated a friend in an emergency – and knowing her knowledge had truly helped – reassured her that she was on the right path.

She threw herself into her studies, foraging for herbs and soaking up everything Miss Powell could teach her. She loved learning about the magic of plants.

Ella hadn't forgotten the golden mirror and Lily, but lately she had been too busy to travel back in time.

That morning, she had planned to forage at the Hermitage, but woke to rain and wind. *Not a day for a walk in the woods,* she thought. Miss Powell was visiting a friend, Scott wasn't scheduled to work, and Ella felt restless after a week indoors.

Her thoughts drifted to Lily and Rose, and she wondered what had been happening in their world. A rainy day felt like the perfect chance to visit.

After breakfast, she climbed to the attic, heart quickening. The ring of keys sat exactly where she'd left them. She chose the gilded mirror key, slid it into the lock, and turned it with a quiet click.

Here goes.

Stepping inside, she closed the door behind her – the world spun – and when the dizziness passed, she pushed the mirror open again.

She was back in the Victorian attic.

Familiar trunks and dust-covered sheets filled the space, but one thing was new: a rail of elegant clothes, both men's and women's, hanging neatly against the wall.

CHAPTER 42

Intrigued, she stepped closer. The fabrics were rich, the stitching exquisite. A green hat with a short brim and embroidered flowers caught her eye. She reached for it - and to her surprise, she could lift it. She placed it where her head should be and felt it settle there.

She tried on a pair of long white gloves; they slid over her hands as if they belonged. In the mirror, the hat and gloves seemed to float - but if she looked closely, she could see the faint outline of her face, hair, and body.

She experimented, adding a long coat. This time, her reflection was clearer, more solid. The more clothing she wore, the more visible she became.

Interesting. Clothes make me solid here.

From downstairs came faint noises. She decided it wouldn't be wise to appear in a house she didn't belong to. Carefully, she removed the clothes, her form fading until she was a simple, invisible presence again.

She drifted downstairs. The house was cold and dim. Only Alison, the maid, was up, moving briskly between the kitchen and drawing room.

Ella followed as Alison raked ashes from the coal fire, carried them outside into the chill, then filled the bucket from the coal bunker. She rebuilt the fire, then moved to the next room, repeating the process.

By now, the bedroom fires would already be lit, Ella realised - meaning Alison had been up before dawn.

When the fires were done, Alison began preparing the kitchen for the day, setting out ingredients, bowls, and pots. Despite coal dust, the room was spotless.

Next, she swept the dining room - which Ella recognised as Miss Powell's apothecary in her own time - and began laying the table for three. A polished oval table sat on a large rug, a sideboard held a decanter of amber liquid and a vase of fresh flowers. The walls were painted light blue, and heavy drapes were drawn across the windows.

Soon, the kitchen filled with the scent of frying bacon and whisked eggs. The family stirred: Lily's father first, then her mother. Mrs Fraser put the kettle on and set the tea tray.

Alison looked up. 'Oh, Mrs Fraser, you didn't have to make the tea. Doesn't feel right, you being in here. I remember when we had a house full of helpers.'

Mrs Fraser smiled faintly. 'Times have changed since the war. I'm only glad we still have you.'

Alison nodded. She knew she was fortunate to still have steady work, even if the days of a full household staff were gone. On Mondays, Mrs Fraser helped with meals and clearing the table to make Alison's long list of chores a little easier.

Aye, thought Alison, *how times have changed.*

Chapter 43

Ella enjoyed watching the household wake up and realised it had been some time since her last visit.

She saw Mr Fraser enter the dining room, where he ate bacon and eggs and drank a cup of tea. He had put on a little weight and wore a suit and tie.

When he finished, he kissed his wife goodbye, put on his overcoat, and headed out the door. 'See you this evening,' he called.

Mrs Fraser and Alison exchanged a smile.

'You know,' said Mrs Fraser, 'that friend of Lily's - Rose - has something special about her. Ever since her first visit here, something changed in Mr Fraser. For the better.'

While Ella had been drifting through the house, taking in the smells and sights of a home from a hundred years ago, she had missed Lily getting up and having breakfast. When she floated into Lily's room, she found her putting on her coat.

'I'm going out now,' Lily called. 'I'll be back after lunch.'

She picked up the keys from the hook in the hall cupboard and headed to the garage to start the car.

Ella, curious about where Lily was going, decided to follow. She remembered the last time she had absorbed her energy into Lily - and how much she enjoyed seeing the world through her eyes.

She floated her energy ahead of Lily and waited. As Lily stepped into the garden and closed the front door, she unknowingly walked straight through Ella.

Immediately, Ella felt herself being absorbed - seeing, hearing, and feeling as if she were Lily. She could even hear Lily's thoughts.

Lily pulled the car from the garage and drove to Morningside Station. She preferred the train to taking the car into the city, enjoying the views along the circular line. Crossing the bridge to the station, she soon boarded a steam train, settling into a seat and watching the countryside blur past.

The journey took her through quiet rural stops before reaching bustling Haymarket, and finally, Waverley Station. Rising with the crowd, she stepped onto the platform.

What a wonderful way to get into the city, Lily thought as she climbed the Waverley steps. At the top, she paused to take in the view.

She never tired of Princes Street. Overlooked by the castle, with gardens on one side and a mix of shops, hotels, and cafés on the other, it was always alive with buses, trams, cars, and pedestrians.

Ella recognised familiar landmarks: the towering Scott Monument to the left and the unfinished monuments of Calton Hill to the right, earning Edinburgh its nickname, the Athens of the North.

Across the street stood Woolworth's department store, opened in 1926 to great fanfare. Lily planned to meet Rose there later for tea in the café, but first, she had an appointment at Jenners Tea Room.

She strolled through the gardens, crossed the street through the stream of trams and cars, and approached Jenners - the grandest department store in Scotland, a Victorian masterpiece.

A doorman opened the double doors, ushering her into a world of polished wood, rich fabrics, and soft lighting. The street noise faded away.

She passed through the perfume and cosmetics department, where elegantly dressed assistants stood behind gleaming counters, offering creams and scents from around the world. Plush chairs invited customers to sit while products were presented with care.

For many ladies, a day at Jenners was an event: shopping, trying on clothes modelled by real women, then enjoying cream tea in the top-floor restaurant before their chauffeur drove them home.

Ella soaked it in - this was Jenners in its prime, a far cry from the modern version competing with chain stores and online shopping.

CHAPTER 43

Lily made her way upstairs and took the lift to the third floor. Stepping out into the tea room, she scanned the room until she spotted her friend waving from a corner table.

Chapter 44

Eager to explore the city for herself, Ella focused her energy on detaching from Lily. She watched as Lily crossed the tearoom to meet her friend, then drifted away, curiosity pulling her elsewhere.

Ella floated out of the tea room and into the store. She found a narrower, dimly lit stairway and wondered where it might lead. She followed it upwards, passing through a door and climbing another set of well-worn steps into a darker, more shadowed part of the building.

This felt like a very different side of Jenners. She recalled reading that, in its heyday, the store had over a hundred rooms and suites for live-in staff. The corridor ahead was silent, and she guessed everyone must be working.

She pushed her energy through a door and into what appeared to be a small attic room. Cracks marked the walls and ceiling. The roof sloped steeply on one side, and a grimy skylight let in only a faint, dusty glow.

Two iron bed frames stood in the centre of the room. One bed was unmade, blankets and sheets twisted as if the occupant had left in a hurry, exposing the thin striped mattress beneath. The other bed was neatly made.

Opposite the beds stood a small fireplace, a table, a chair, and a clothes horse. The space was sparse - a cleaner's or kitchen maid's quarters, Ella guessed.

She drifted out, down the stairs, and along another corridor. Here, a door opened onto a much larger room. A double wooden-framed bed stood under a window dressed with warm drapes. A rug lay in the centre of the floor, and the fireplace was adorned with a mantelpiece holding a vase of fresh flowers.

The room was well furnished: wardrobe, sofa, a standing mirror in the

CHAPTER 44

corner, a desk and a chair. The walls were painted pale blue, with framed prints hanging neatly. From the care in the décor, Ella thought this must belong to a higher-paid shop assistant.

Clothes lay neatly across the bed - confirming it was a woman's room - and gave Ella an idea. She slipped a satin top over her head and glanced in the mirror. The soft fabric skimmed her frame, revealing a faint outline of the rest of her body.

She pulled on a wide pair of satin trousers, shoes, an outer coat, white gloves, and a wide-brimmed hat. Whatever these clothes were, they were stylish - flowing and elegant. She reached out to touch the furniture, delighted to find she could.

Spinning on the spot, she laughed aloud. She tucked her long hair under the hat as best she could, then pulled a face in the mirror, sticking out her tongue and grinning.

Oh, what an adventure she was going to have now - walking through old Edinburgh as if she truly belonged there.

Chapter 45

Miss Powell, upon her return to the house, wondered where Ella was. They had arranged to do some studying that afternoon. She called out, but there was no answer. She even opened the door at the bottom of the attic stairs and called out, 'Ella, are you there?' Still, no answer.

Oh well, she thought, *she must have gone out after all.* She stepped into her study and took a good look around. So many years of history in this room. She was glad to have it open and in use again. There was so much precious knowledge here, and it was only right to share it with the new generation.

She sat on the leather chair and drifted away. She had spent so many days, weeks, and years in this room and had hundreds of people come through the door with their aches, pains, and problems. She had to admit that she missed those days. Perhaps it was time to open up her apothecary again.

Whilst Miss Powell reminisced about the old days, Ella was actually living in the old days! She was now fully dressed and solid in 1920s Edinburgh. She made her way down the stairs, back into the public part of the department store.

Ella walked through the ladies' fashion department, taking it all in. It was dedicated to ladies' fashion. There were dresses displayed on mannequins arranged elegantly throughout the room.

Hanging from large brass rails were other beautiful dresses. The shop assistants stood behind their highly polished counters, elegantly dressed and made up, either chatting with each other or helping a customer choose her next dress.

The displays and atmosphere of this department were so elegant, tempting,

CHAPTER 45

and beautiful. Ella could have spent hours there, but she knew she didn't have that much time.

She made her way downstairs, past the cosmetic counters she had passed earlier, and loved it when the doorman opened the door for her and said, 'Good afternoon.' This confirmed to her that she was solid and could be seen in this world.

Ella stepped onto the world-famous Princes Street. Though she had walked it countless times before, she had never honestly stopped to take in its magnificence. Maybe it was because it was her hometown, so familiar that she often overlooked its beauty – but in this moment, she saw it with fresh eyes.

She had always thought that Princes Street was nice. After all, how could it not be? It's overlooked by the magnificent castle, has beautiful gardens, and some of the original architecture and landmarks make it still very picturesque. However, in her time, the street was lined with mobile phone shops, budget department stores, and shoe shops.

But oh, what a different place Princes Street was in those days. She stepped onto the busy street. Smartly dressed men and women, all seemingly with great purpose, were walking in all directions. The newspaper stand was busy with people buying their daily Evening News.

As Ella glanced up and down Princes Street, so many familiar landmarks stood before her – the towering Walter Scott Monument, the grand Art Gallery at the Mound, and the lovely gardens stretching below. But one thing caught her eye – where the Waverley shopping centre should have been, there was nothing but a rooftop garden, dotted with benches, flower beds, and neatly trimmed grass. In her mind, it looked so much better than the modern building that was there now.

She was charmed by the elegance of the people's dresses as they went about their everyday business. Men dressed in suits and ties, women wearing dresses, coats, hats, and gloves – with a few, like her, wearing wide satin trousers. These ordinary people, going about their business, had no idea how stylish they looked to her.

She stepped back towards the entrance of Jenners and, to her surprise, saw

Lily coming down the steps.

'Oh no.' Ella felt slightly panicked. 'I thought I had plenty of time.'

She wasn't quite sure what to do. She didn't want to lose Lily. But then she remembered that Lily had said she was going to meet Rose at Woolworth's café, so she knew where Lily would be. Lily was her anchor in this time and place, and Ella didn't want to be too far away from her.

She rushed back into Jenners and, as elegantly as she could, walked quickly through the different departments until she found the stairs that led to the room from which she had borrowed the clothes.

She gently knocked on the door, hoping there would be no one in. There was no reply. She pushed the door open gently and was relieved to find it as she had left it.

She took one last look at herself in the mirror. She did look rather chic, she had to admit, as she admired the stylish clothes she was wearing.

She then removed her clothes layer by layer. As she removed an item, the outline of her body would fade.

She laid the clothes out as she had found them and turned around to look at her reflection again. Well, there was no reflection of her. She had become a ball of invisible energy again.

In this form, she could move much more quickly and even through walls. She floated straight out a window and down to Princes Street, along to the East End, where she knew Woolworths store was.

She didn't have time to take in her surroundings. She was too focused on finding Lily.

She floated through the doors at Woolworth's, noting there was no doorman here like there was in Jenners, and saw a sign pointing to the café upstairs.

She floated up the stairs to the large café. In her mind, it was still elegant for a Woolworth's café, but it didn't carry the opulence or dignified atmosphere of the tea room in Jenners.

Ella saw Lily sitting down, and opposite her was Rose, the forager and healer.

Chapter 46

The two women exchanged a warm hug before settling at the table, ready for tea and cake. Ella had a feeling they'd be deep in conversation for a while, giving her the perfect chance to explore.

Excitement bubbled within her at the thought of seeing Woolworths as it was a hundred years ago. Seizing the opportunity, she drifted back downstairs into the vast store, eager to take it all in. There was so much to look at. Wooden signs said, *Nothing is over 6d.* The shop floor was jam-packed with people, and there were so many items for sale.

As she floated down an aisle, the wooden cabinets and shelves on one side displayed rolls and rolls of material, laces, and ribbons. Further along, they transitioned to rolls of linoleum and carpets, along with everything needed to accompany a purchase - tools, tape, and a variety of other items.

In the middle aisle were pots, pans, lids, baking trays, and every kitchen accessory you could imagine.

The store cleverly kept everything under 6d by charging for items separately. Ella noticed that a good-sized kitchen pot was 5d and its lid was 2d. *The beginnings of clever marketing,* she thought.

As she floated through the store, she saw every imaginable item needed for the home and garden.

Near the front of the store, shiny glass counters displayed every type of jewellery, makeup, and cosmetics. There was a spectacular Pic N Mix sweet display and a large stand of garden bulbs and tools.

Customers bustled across the shop floor, picking up goods and buying as they went. The atmosphere was very different from the dignified air of

Jenners' store. Woolworths was busy, noisy, and buzzing with the excitement of bargain-hunting.

Much as Ella would have loved to stay and see more, she realised she should get back to Lily and Rose.

She floated up to the café, admiring the simple Art Deco design. She saw Lily and floated over to her and Rose, close enough to hear their conversation.

'Good, that's settled then,' said Lily, her face glowing with excitement. 'When Mother and Father move to the countryside next month, you'll rent the house from us - with the option to buy in the future.' She leaned in, eager to share the news with Rose. 'It makes perfect sense. I'll be living at the hospital full-time for my work, and we want the house to go to a growing family who will truly appreciate it. I know you and your family will love it just as much as we have.'

Rose went to say something, but Lily didn't give her a chance.

'And no, Rose, please don't argue about the rental price. We have what we need, and our family wants the house to go to people who will love it like we did and make it their home.'

Rose's expression was pure joy. 'You cannot begin to imagine how this will change our lives, Lily. Having such a beautiful home and a space where I can share my practice with others would be amazing. And a garden to grow my plants and herbs!'

'But,' continued Rose, 'I do worry about my current neighbours and how I can continue to see them; they are so important to me.'

'Well, we shall have to come up with an imaginative way to make that happen. Where there's a will, there's a way.'

Rose had found that to be true ever since meeting Lily. When her friend put her mind to something, things happened. Lily was a powerhouse of action, and with her on her side, Rose had begun to believe anything was possible.

Fascinated, Ella floated closer to hear more.

'Rose, what you've done for my father has changed all of our lives.' Lily's voice softened. 'We're so grateful for the time you spent with him, the special herbs and tinctures you made, and the many walks foraging for the right plants and herbs you know he needed. I know you gave a great deal of your

CHAPTER 46

time and energy to his healing. He wouldn't see anyone before. My mother and I are so happy to see him working, whistling, and interested in life again.' Lily paused, looking at Rose with admiration.

'It's amazing, the difference in him. He still has flashbacks, but now he copes with them – and it's without a doubt thanks to you, Rose. What you did goes beyond any payment I could give you. You've given him back his life, and in doing that, you've given my mother hers back, too. You're looking for a new house, and we're looking for someone to take over ours, so it works out for everyone.'

Rose blushed and said she would have done the same for anyone, but thanked Lily for her kind words.

My goodness, thought Ella, *what have I missed?* While she had been so busy in her own time and space, so much had happened here as well. Or perhaps she had stepped out into a different time zone entirely. She had no idea what year it was.

It was news to her that Lily was going to live at the asylum – and that her parents were moving to the country, leaving the house for Rose to move into.

The ladies finished their tea, and Rose grabbed Lily's hand. 'Thank you so much for taking this leap of faith in me. I'm so pleased you followed your dreams and are now a psychiatric nurse at the asylum.'

The two friends hugged again and walked downstairs onto the shop floor.

'I have a few things to pick up whilst I'm here,' Rose said. 'It was lovely to see you, Lily. Please give my best wishes to your mother and father.'

'Of course I will. They'll be happy to know you're keeping well and delighted that you and your family want to take over the house. I'll keep in touch and we'll soon have a date for you to move.'

'That will be lovely.' Rose hesitated, looked at Lily intently and said, 'My life changed the day you knocked on my door. Thank you for all that you do for us.' With a lovely smile, she disappeared into the throng of Woolworths shoppers.

Lily stepped out onto the East End of Princes Street and glanced at the clock on the North British Hotel – the largest railway hotel outside London, with a clock tower visible along the entire street.

It was five minutes to three. Lily hurried down Waverley Steps to catch the 3 p.m. train to Morningside.

Ella kept close on the journey back. She loved sitting on the train, watching old Edinburgh pass by.

The train trundled into Morningside Station. Lily stepped off, crossed the busy road crowded with trams, cars, and people, then got into her car and drove home.

How interesting that Lily's parents were moving to the country. Mr Fraser must be much better to make such a big move, and for Rose and her family to move into the big house from such a tiny flat was a massive change.

But the news that excited Ella the most was that Lily was now a fully qualified psychiatric nurse, living in the hospital, with time to study to become a psychiatrist. Ella felt incredibly proud of Lily for following her passion and dreams of working with patients.

Ella enjoyed the drive back, watching the familiar neighbourhood of a time gone by. When Lily put the car into the garage, Ella silently said goodbye and floated upstairs to the attic, ready to return to her own time.

The attic felt still, as if the golden mirror was waiting for her. As she stepped closer, the familiar pull took hold, drawing her towards it. Floating into the cupboard behind the mirror, she readied herself for the transition. Moments later, she was home – back in her own time, yet the past still clung to her, as real as the present moment.

Chapter 47

Still in the attic, Ella sat back against the old wooden floorboards, her heart racing from everything she had just experienced.

Then, a thrill of realisation washed over her – she had witnessed the very moment that shaped Miss Powell's family connection to the house. At last, the fragments of history were beginning to fall into place. Rose's knowledge of healing and herbs, her life in the very house that now belonged to Miss Powell – it was all connected. The intricate threads of the past and present were weaving together before her eyes.

And then it struck her – Rose wasn't just any healer. She was Miss Powell's mother.

Ella would love to hear Miss Powell's childhood tales. More than that, she could feel the past reaching out and touching the present day. Surprisingly, she felt a stronger bond with Lily than with anyone in her own life - except perhaps Miss Powell. Despite Lily living more than a century ago, Ella saw her as a mentor and guiding force in her current life.

As Ella descended the attic stairs, she nearly bumped into Miss Powell.

'Ah, lass, there you are. I've been looking for you,' said Miss Powell. 'I called out earlier and got no response. I thought you had gone out. Have you been up there all this time?'

Ella found herself in a dilemma. She didn't want to lie to Miss Powell, but she wasn't sure what to say. 'Actually, I was up there most of the day. I don't even know what time it is now,' she admitted, a bit flustered. She heard the distant hum of the lawnmower.

'Is that Scott out there?' Ella asked, trying to change the subject. 'I forgot it was his day to come.'

Miss Powell stepped aside, studying Ella intently. She sensed that Ella couldn't have been in the attic all afternoon. She had called up the stairs twice without any response. She could tell just by looking at Ella that she was flustered and holding something back.

'Well,' she thought, 'whatever is going on, I'm sure she will tell me in her own time.' Her trust in Ella was complete, but it didn't stop her from wondering.

In the garden, Scott hoped to catch a glimpse of Ella. He had seen her in a different light the day she tended to him after his accident. Unknown to Ella, he had fallen a bit deeper for her on that day. He kept replaying the moment when he opened his eyes, found her looking at him, and felt that unexpected connection.

Feeling guilty for making Miss Powell search for her, Ella couldn't shake off the awareness that she was getting too absorbed in the past and neglecting the present. Miss Powell had been a great mentor, imparting knowledge about herbs and their magical properties and generously sharing her skills.

Since Ella became Miss Powell's student - exploring the apothecary and learning about herbs - she had felt she'd found her life's path. Reflecting on Lily, she felt she was drawing inspiration from her to focus on her own life, intentions, and goals.

Despite enjoying her work and studies, Ella felt that something was missing. She could almost hear her sister Janey saying she needed more fun. Walking into the garden to clear her head, Ella decided to prioritise what was important to her, shake off the past, and take charge of her life.

Taking a deep breath, Ella admired the warm, sunny day and the vibrant garden. Seeing Scott working, she felt a pleasant anticipation, and she slowly walked over to him. He had already noticed her emerging from the house.

Miss Powell observed Ella and Scott from the window, sensing the sparks of attraction between them. She wondered when they would act on it.

The trouble with youth, thought Miss Powell, *is that it's wasted on the young.* She smiled, reminiscing about the confusing emotions of being young.

The doorbell rang. Miss Powell anticipated that if it were a regular visitor,

CHAPTER 47

they would come around the side of the house soon enough; if a stranger, they would ring again. A few minutes later, Janey appeared at the door, looking for Ella.

'She's busy outside right now, Janey. Come in and take a seat. It's always nice to see a young face around here,' Miss Powell said.

Janey seemed uncomfortable without Ella around. Miss Powell observed a change in Janey's usual confident attitude. She sensed an underlying sadness and uncertainty beneath Janey's exterior. She contemplated the differences between the two sisters. Ella wore her heart on her sleeve, while Janey hid hers behind a carefree mask. Though she had never spoken of any troubles, Miss Powell could sense Janey's inner turmoil.

She looked at Janey again, realising that behind her lively persona, there was more to the story. Ella, on the other hand, seemed to be holding something back lately, a subtle shift Miss Powell couldn't quite pinpoint.

Janey hadn't spent time alone with Miss Powell or in this room before. Ella had often spoken fondly about her - her stories, her quirky humour, and her tarot readings. Janey let herself settle into the comfy chair and admired the room, letting herself relax; the space and Miss Powell seemed to have that effect on her. Her eyes wandered to the purple cloth, under which she knew from Ella's stories lay the ancient tarot cards.

Janey admitted to herself that she was intrigued by Miss Powell and would love to have a reading from her. She was feeling a bit down and confused about whether she was being honest with herself.

Miss Powell could sense that all was not well. She also suspected Janey wasn't the type to take advice directly. She saw her glance at the silk-covered tarot cards.

'Would you like a card reading whilst you wait for Ella? I think she's talking to Scott right now, and it looks like they will be deep in conversation for a while.'

Janey shifted in her seat. 'Aye, I think I would. Well, I know I would.'

'Have a wee think about what you want to focus on. You can tell me if you like, or you can keep it in mind when you hold the cards.' Miss Powell slowly unwrapped the silk cloth and picked up the cards, holding them to her heart.

'Now, come a wee bit closer, Janey. Have a seat just here.' Miss Powell patted the sofa next to her and moved a small table between them. 'Give the cards a wee shuffle, focus on what you want the cards to help you with. I want the cards to feel your energy, and when you're ready, put them back on the table.'

Janey picked up the cards gently and moved them around. The cards felt good in her hands. She focused on her boyfriend as she did this. She was intrigued by what she might learn. She didn't mean to speak out loud, but she did.

'Is Rab the right guy for me?' She had a feeling she knew the answer, but wanted reassurance. She laid the cards down.

'Divide the cards into three piles, and then bring them all together into one pile.'

Janey followed the instructions. Miss Powell picked up the cards, held them close to her heart, closed her eyes for a moment and said, 'Whatever the cards say, the future's not set in stone. You have complete control over your life. The cards are not here to tell you what you should do, but to help you see things differently. They are not here to tell you the future, but to guide you - if you allow them.'

'I think a three card reading will be perfect for you, my dear, unless the cards say I need to turn over more.' She peeled off the top three cards. All were Major Arcana - the most powerful cards in the deck.

The cards on the table were The Moon, The Devil, and The Tower. Janey wasn't familiar with tarot cards, but the images struck her as beautiful and powerful. Miss Powell took a deep breath. To have three Major Arcana in such a simple reading was unusual, and she knew they had a strong message for Janey.

'These are all very powerful cards, my dear. Let's begin with the Moon card. This card suggests you are living in the shadows, not fully embracing life or revealing your true potential. The Moon tells us that nothing is what it seems. You present one face to the world, but your true feelings remain hidden. Now let's see how this relates to your boyfriend.'

'You feel he is only showing one side to you, and you sense a darker, hidden

CHAPTER 47

side. Sometimes you can't be your true self around him, and you tread carefully at times.'

Janey listened closely, drawn in by the ritual and the meaning.

'But the Moon is also positive – it symbolises the feminine within us. You have the power to harness this. To move forward and upward, consider letting go of what no longer serves you. Does this make sense?'

Janey took a deep breath, tears in her eyes. 'Aye, it does. Please, go on.'

'The next card is The Devil. It shows the ancient goat god holding a man and a woman captive with chains. It can look frightening, especially to those unfamiliar with the Tarot. This tells me there is someone in your life who is selfish, controlling, and possibly caught up in addictions. They want to control all relationships. But look at the chains – they are loose. We often place these chains on ourselves, and we can remove them too.'

'Are you alright, my dear? Do you want me to continue?'

Janey nodded silently. Tears flowed down her face. Miss Powell gave her a tissue and waited.

'Thank you. I'm okay. Please go on,' said Janey. 'The final card represents where the relationship is going.' They both looked at The Tower – crumbling to the ground, a figure diving from the top. 'I'm listening,' said Janey. 'The Tower represents destruction and chaos. It warns that things you thought were strong can suddenly fall – relationships, beliefs, even self-perception. But it can also bring revelation and awakening. After a breakdown, you can rebuild, stronger and wiser. Sometimes a bolt out of the blue frees us from what holds us back.'

She let the words sink in. Janey sat with her shoulders slumped, taking it all in. The reading hadn't surprised her. She already knew the truth.

She straightened up, blew her nose, and thanked Miss Powell for the reading.

Chapter 48

Miss Powell watched as Janey went into the garden and spoke with her sister. Scott stepped away to give them space. He could see Janey was upset and didn't want to get between the sisters.

'What's going on with you, Janey? You look like you haven't slept for days,' said Ella, upset to see her sister looking so worn down. She suspected things were far from fine, despite the happy mask Janey wore. Ella had always thought her boyfriend was a nasty piece of work and had never liked him. Ever since Janey and Rab had got together, he seemed intent on bringing her down and trying to control her.

Janey was usually confident, but somehow she always ended up with men who mistreated her.

'Is everything okay with you and Rab? You know what I think of him, Janey. He is not a good man. He doesn't treat you well,' said Ella. They didn't always see eye to eye, but she hated to see anyone mistreat her sister.

'Aye, I'm beginning to see he's not the right guy for me,' admitted Janey, to Ella's surprise and relief. At last, her sister was coming to her senses. 'I've made up my mind: I am going to leave him. I know it's not a healthy relationship - as you've told me so many times - and I just haven't been listening. I'm going to start looking for somewhere else to live and then move out without telling him, because he will just go mental and try to stop me.'

Ella didn't like the idea of Janey stalling. She was worried for her 'Why wait, Janey? You know you can move back to Mum's if you need to. I know it's not ideal, but she would be happy to take you in. And why wait? Listen - I'll help

CHAPTER 48

you move out, and I'm sure if we ask Scott nicely, we can use his van. We could even move you out today,' said Ella. She hesitated, wanting to find the right words. She had a sense that if Janey didn't move out now, she might lose the determination needed to see this through.

'Leaving isn't going to get easier the longer you stay. Rab needs to be in control of every situation - and of you, Janey. You know it's true,' pleaded Ella. She knew her sister's patterns. Janey put on a blustery, extroverted front, broadcasting that everything was shiny and good, but deep down, she was allowing herself to be controlled and bullied by her so-called boyfriend.

The thought scared Ella. If she didn't do something now, something terrible might happen. She also realised she hadn't seen Janey for a while and had neglected to check in. She had been so caught up in her studies, foraging, and visiting her mentors behind the golden mirror that she was ashamed to admit Janey had slipped to the back of her mind.

But Janey could be exhausting. She always wanted to party or go out, never talking about her feelings - always putting on that *Look at me, I'm fine* act. And Ella knew she wasn't fine.

It wasn't that Ella had given up, but there were only so many times you could offer to help someone who wouldn't help themselves.

'I'll be all right for a couple of weeks. I won't tell him a thing, and in the meantime, I'll find a room or a flat. Then I'll move out when he's working and that will be that,' said Janey, her brave face slipping back into place.

Ella called Scott over. 'Scott, you know Rab - Janey's boyfriend - don't you?'

Scott put down his gardening tools and walked over. 'I know of him,' said Scott. 'He's not someone I'd choose to hang out with, to be honest. I've heard stories about him and his brother - and it's not a good reputation.'

He looked at Janey, his expression serious. 'He's bad news. I'm not just saying that. He's known for mistreating girlfriends. And you must know by now - he doesn't just take heavy drugs - he and his brother deal them all over Leith. They don't care about anyone but themselves. One of their scams is buying prescription drugs from people looking for street stuff, then selling them at a huge profit to anyone desperate enough to pay.'

Scott wondered how much to tell Janey but decided it was only fair to share what he knew.

'He's always getting off his face and making an arse of himself up the town. When I tried telling you that before, it wasn't because I was making a move on you, it was because you're Ella's sister and you deserve better.'

Janey flushed with embarrassment, remembering when she had come on to Scott. She had just been trying to feel attractive again.

'If you ever need a hand moving out, Janey, I'd be happy to help - along with Ella, of course,' he said, smiling over at Ella, wanting her to know he'd be there for both of them.

'Thanks,' Janey said sheepishly. 'Maybe in a week or two when I get myself sorted, but thanks.'

She turned to leave, but Ella grabbed her arm. 'Janey, if you change your mind and decide to leave sooner, call me and I'll be there.'

'Aye, thanks,' said Janey. 'I'll keep you posted about finding somewhere else to live. I'm away now. I know what I need to do,' she said, more to herself than Ella.

She waved at Miss Powell through the living room window and took off up the hill to catch the bus.

Chapter 49

When Janey returned to the flat she shared with Rab - just a few days after her last visit to Ella and Miss Powell - she took a long, hard look at her surroundings. It was his flat she had moved into, and she had never truly felt it was her home.

The flat was dark, dingy, messy, and masculine. Now, looking at it with clear eyes, she saw it for what it was - a depressing, dark environment.

It was crammed with Rab's stuff, and he complained whenever she tried to make even subtle changes to make it feel homely. Being a basement flat, there was very little natural light.

At the start, she had thought it was a cool pad - a bit of a party den. Most weekends, it was the place to hang out and get wasted before going out, or to pile back into at 4 a.m. after the pubs and clubs closed.

Because Janey had been so busy partying and enjoying playing the part of Rab's girlfriend in front of his mates, she had ignored how she truly felt about the flat - and the life she was living. Fueled by the highs and lows of alcohol and recreational drugs, she convinced herself she was happy.

But now, she felt like her eyes had been opened - to her living situation and to her relationship with Rab. The tarot reading from Miss Powell had made her see things differently, and it wasn't looking good. Rab's temperament seemed to be getting worse, and she felt like she was constantly walking on eggshells.

He drank, smoked, and got high when he wasn't working. Janey was relieved when he left for his night shifts five nights a week - at least then she had space to herself.

He always left her a big bag of grass and a couple of Valium 'to chill out,' he said. At first, she thought it was cool. Sometimes she'd invite a friend over, open a bottle of wine, get smashed, and fall into bed. But recently, she had spent the evenings alone - smoking joints, taking Valium, sipping Jack Daniels, and crawling into bed wasted.

The past couple of nights, she had cut back. She knew she needed a clearer head to find somewhere else to live. Allowing herself to be honest, she finally admitted she wasn't happy - and had to do something about it.

She had been searching for other places to live, keeping her search a secret from Rab. Tonight was his night off, and he'd gone out earlier. She didn't know where, only that he had slammed the door and barked, 'Just be here when I get back.'

Janey picked up her phone and opened her email, hoping for replies to the ads she had answered.

A knock came at the door. She closed her email, not wanting to leave it open, and walked down the short hall.

Rab's friend Ronnie barged past her.

'He's not here right now, Ronnie, ' Janey called after him as he headed for the living room.

'I'll wait. Beer in the fridge?' he asked, like he lived there. Ronnie was a big guy with a nasty streak, so Janey didn't argue.

'Aye, help yourself,' she said, closing the living room door behind him.

She went into the bedroom, checked her phone - still no messages. She glanced around at the mess.

Under the bed, she had started hiding small, packed items. The more she could prepare without him knowing, the quicker she could escape.

Another knock. *Jeez, who is that now?*

She opened the door - Rab stood there. His eyes were dark, menacing. Whisky fumes hit her before he spoke. He looked high and out of control.

She stepped back to let him in, murmuring, 'Oh, hi.' Rab stormed into the hall, shoved her against the wall and kicked the door closed.

He grabbed her shoulders and head-butted her. Janey heard a sickening crack, felt her nose explode, and blood gushing down her face.

CHAPTER 49

He slammed her against the wall again and kneed her in the ribs. She slid down, gasping, but he yanked her back up by her neck, thumbs digging into her throat until she could barely breathe.

Just before she thought her eyes would burst, he let go. She collapsed. He kicked her in the stomach as she curled up.

Surely Ronnie will come out and help? But no one came.

Rab left her crumpled in the hall and slammed the living room door behind him.

Janey had no idea what had triggered the attack. She touched her face - her hand came away bloody. Her breathing was ragged, painful.

She staggered into the bathroom, grabbed a towel, caught sight of her face, sobbed - and ran.

She stumbled out of the flat, down the steps, and sat crying. Blood dripped onto her clothes. She pressed the towel to her face.

No phone. No way she'd go back in.

She climbed to the street. It was dark and quiet. People glanced at her, horrified. A young girl asked if she could help. Janey just shook her head and kept walking, sobbing.

She slumped on the steps of a closed shop, head in her hands, unsure how long she sat there.

A shadow fell over her. 'You okay, lass?'

She looked up to see a policeman and a policewoman. 'Come on, we'll take you to the hospital,' the policeman said. Janey froze. She didn't want the hospital or the police. Rab had drugs in the flat - would that somehow get her in trouble?

The policewoman knelt beside her. 'If your partner did this, we won't take you back to him. You can report it after you're checked over.'

'I'm alright. Just leave me,' Janey sobbed.

'We can't leave you here. Do you have family nearby?'

Janey hesitated, then gave Ella's address. She couldn't face her mum like this.

They eased her into the car, asking again if she wanted hospital or to report. She refused.

'You know you can report later,' the policewoman said gently. 'Whoever did this should not get away with it.'

Janey pressed the blood-soaked towel to her face, still wondering what the hell had just happened – and why.

Chapter 50

The next day, Miss Powell sat in her living room, holding her tarot cards against her chest. She could feel their energy flowing into her palms.

She had heard the police arriving late last night and delivering Janey to Ella. Very little happened in the house that she didn't know about. When she'd read the cards for Janey, she'd seen the signs of an exceptionally troubled relationship - but she took no satisfaction in being right.

That morning, Ella had been as subtle as she could, offering a softened version of events: Rab had hit Janey, and could she stay for a few days? Miss Powell had agreed, 'Yes, but only for a few days.' Ella had looked relieved and gone back to tend to her sister.

Miss Powell suspected that Ella was shielding her from the full truth, perhaps thinking she was too delicate to hear the worst of it. But that girl has no idea what I have seen in my lifetime, she thought. She doesn't know the stories I've heard, the injuries I've helped heal, or the damage I've seen one person inflict upon another.

If Ella knew the extent of her healing past, she would realise there was no need to protect her. But to be fair, Ella had no way of knowing.

Miss Powell had not yet seen Janey, but from the drawn, weary look on Ella's face, she could only imagine. Janey had arrived in the middle of the night, accompanied by the police, fleeing from whatever horrors had driven her there.

Miss Powell was certain that, no matter the hour, some neighbours would have noticed the visit from the police. This was still a street where nothing escaped notice, and she had seen her fair share of late-night knocks at the door – often from women needing help after trouble in their own homes.

Her mind wandered back to the days when she was well-known as a healer, and her house had been a haven for those seeking herbs, tinctures, or a quiet ear. She had tended to neighbours and strangers alike. Money or a grand house made no difference; grief, pain, and trouble came to all. Miss Powell understood this better than most.

Whatever was said in her study stayed there. She neither gossiped nor suffered fools gladly. Her reputation for skill and discretion had travelled far.

It had not been easy being the sounding board for so many. In her younger years, the weight of others' pain sometimes made her feel as if her head would burst.

She missed her mother deeply – especially having someone to share her day with. They had been like two peas in a pod, a perfect team. Even decades later, she thought of her daily.

Her knowledge of healing and herbs, passed down from her mother, still lived within her. She felt it was time to share it again – and perhaps Ella was the one to carry it forward. The next few days would reveal whether her young companion had a true gift for healing.

Chapter 51

Ella was in the kitchen putting the kettle on, thinking about how quickly life could change - often in ways far beyond one's control. Until last night, she had been settling into a lovely rhythm with Miss Powell. She still took care of her everyday work around the house, but now she was also spending time studying and picking herbs with Miss Powell's guidance. She was a fountain of knowledge, teaching Ella in a way that made every lesson fascinating.

She knew she was lucky to have been taken under Miss Powell's wing. For the first time in a long while, Ella felt she had found a path that truly suited her.

And if that wasn't exciting enough, she sensed a spark between herself and Scott - maybe he did like her. She was almost ready to do something about it.

Then, in the middle of the night, Janey had turned up at her door with a broken nose, injured ribs, and a crushed spirit. Life wasn't quite the same this morning.

Of course, Ella felt for Janey. But there was a part of her that was angry too - angry that Janey had stayed with Rab when it was obvious, at least to Ella, that it was an unhealthy relationship. Even so, she had to admit she'd never imagined he would turn violent.

Miss Powell had agreed that Janey could stay a few days while she recovered. Ella knew how private the Miss Powell was, so even that was pushing her out of her comfort zone. Ella was determined not to take advantage; she valued her life here far too much to risk upsetting the balance.

She was making tea for Janey and Miss Powell when she cracked open the side door to let in some fresh air before the evening turned cold. As she did, she heard the side garden gate close. Someone was outside.

That's odd, she thought. There shouldn't be anyone out there at this time. It was early evening, the sky beginning to darken. She opened the door fully and stepped out.

A sudden presence loomed. Before she could react, a hand clamped onto her shoulder and spun her around.

Ella instantly recognised Janey's ex-boyfriend, Rab.

'What the hell are you doing here?' she demanded.

Rab was big all over - broad shoulders, six-foot-two, with dark hair scraped into a ponytail. His skin was pasty, his close-set brown eyes cold and mean. A pointy nose and thin, hard lips gave him a permanently unpleasant expression. He carried extra weight around his middle, mostly hidden by his height. A leather jacket, jeans, and black boots completed the look.

Ella had only met him once before, but once seen, he was impossible to forget. He radiated menace.

'I know she's here. Get Janey out here now,' he growled, shoving Ella up against the wall.

She caught the stale stench of alcohol on his breath. His pupils were pinpricks, his eyes glittering with hostility. Inside, Ella's stomach lurched, but anger flared hotter than fear. She twisted out from under his grip and shoved him back.

'You should be locked up, you bastard.' Her voice was calm and steady, belying the adrenaline coursing through her. 'You're nothing but a scumbag. What gives you the right to be here?'

Her eyes stayed fixed on him, unblinking.

'What the hell do you think hitting a woman proves? That you're tough? That you've got power?' She let the silence stretch before delivering the final blow. 'You're nothing but a bully. A coward. A joke of a man.'

He stared at her, taken aback. Most people cowered under his intimidation, but this woman stood her ground. He straightened to his full height.

'I don't know who the fuck you think you are,' he said, low and dangerous, 'but no one talks to me like that. I know Janey's here - tell her to come the fuck home, or I'll come in and drag her out.'

CHAPTER 51

Ella didn't flinch. She took a step back, creating space, and pulled her phone from her pocket.

'I'm giving you twenty seconds to get away from this door, Rab Johnstone. Janey's not here – I don't know where she is, but she's not here. Turn around and walk away, or I'll call the police and report you for trespassing.' She tapped her screen. 'And I'm sure they'd be delighted to search you and your house for whatever drugs you've got stashed.'

Rab hesitated, surprised at her defiance. She was nothing like her sister.

'I'm no pushover, you big bully. Get away from here and don't come back. If I see your face around here again, I'll call the police. I'm not afraid of a woman-beater like you.'

Something in her calm certainty made him step back. He knew she meant every word.

'I'll find her,' he muttered, though without conviction. The pocketful of Valium and speed in his jacket made him wary of sticking around.

Ella watched as he climbed into his car and drove off.

Only then did she let out a long breath, leaning against the wall as adrenaline surged through her veins. Rage bubbled at the thought that he'd had the audacity to show up here. How had he even found out where she lived?

She took another deep breath before stepping back inside, more shaken than she wanted to admit.

Chapter 52

Miss Powell sat in the living room, looking out the window and appreciating the beautiful morning. She didn't like that a violent, unpredictable man had shown up at her house last night. Unknown to Ella, she had been perched in her study, overhearing everything happening outside. Her phone was ready in her hand, 999 already in mind, in case the situation spiralled out of control.

In the end, she hadn't needed to call. Miss Powell had learned something new about Ella - she hadn't known that Ella could be that feisty. She was proud of her. Still, the time had come: something had to be done. This was their home, their safe space, and having Janey here made life unpredictable and potentially dangerous for them all.

Just then, Ella nudged open the living room door with her shoulder, balancing a tea tray, and set it down on the stool.

'Morning, Miss Powell. It's a beautiful day out there today,' Ella chirped, still unaware that Miss Powell knew about Rab's late-night visit.

'Morning, Ella. Aye, that it is.' The tea was poured, and Miss Powell waited. Usually, she would bring Ella up to date with the day's news or offer her a reading, but this morning she sat quietly, sipping.

This was a crucial moment for her student, though she wasn't sure Ella realised it.

Meanwhile, on the other side of the house, Janey stirred in the small guest room - a cosy space with a comfortable single bed, thick curtains, and a big window overlooking evergreen trees. Birdsong drifted in through the glass. She was grateful to be alive, grateful simply to be here.

It had been three days since the attack. Her body still ached from the kicks

CHAPTER 52

to her ribs and stomach. She touched her nose and the skin around her eyes. Still tender, but better.

She hadn't cried much in those days. Well - if she were honest, she'd cried that first morning when she looked in the mirror.

Ella hadn't allowed her near a mirror the night she'd arrived. Instead, she'd swept her into what looked like an apothecary straight from a film set, a room Janey hadn't even known existed in the old house. She'd been settled in a comfortable chair, cleaned up, given herbal tea and tinctures, soothing gel on her face and body. Ella had run her a bath, helped her undress, and left her to soak. When she returned, she brought fresh, fluffy pyjamas and helped Janey into them.

It had been oddly comforting, letting Ella take control without asking questions she wasn't ready to answer.

That first morning, the mirror showed her the damage: eyes swollen and purple, nose bent slightly out of shape with a cut across the bridge, a small chip in her front tooth. She'd shed a few tears, but refused to let herself sob - fearing she wouldn't stop. She still didn't understand what had triggered the attack.

Through the days that followed, Ella continued to be an angel. She dressed Janey's wounds, iced her nose and eyes, and gave her Arnica every couple of hours. She'd made a herbal comfrey solution from her own garden to soak gauze for Janey's face, ribs, and stomach. There was Arnica gel for bruises, parsley leaves crushed and laid over her eyes, St John's Wort tea brewed daily from flowers Ella had picked and dried herself. She'd even made oil from the plant, dabbing it gently on Janey's bruises alongside doses of Vitamin K.

And through it all - no questions, no 'I told you so.'

This morning, Janey stood before the mirror again. The swelling had gone down considerably. The bruises had shifted from dark purples to lighter greens and yellows. Her ribs still hurt, but she was healing.

Her body felt halfway to normal, but her mind was another matter. She kept replaying the attack in her head.

Still, she felt a flicker of control returning. Shame burned in her - she couldn't believe she'd let this happen. She thought maybe it was time to get out of this guest room and back to her life.

But she also hated to admit she was missing the nightly cocktail of downers and joints Rab had always supplied, along with the coke or speed for when she needed to be brought back up again. She could see now it was a way to keep her hooked, but her body still craved it.

She didn't miss him - but she wasn't quite ready to give up the drugs. A few downers, a few big joints, would smooth things over nicely.

Ella knew nothing about that part of her life. The herbs were helping her body, but inside, Janey felt that itch that only drugs could scratch. She made up her mind.

She stepped into the shower, letting warm water wash over her. Slowly, she lathered her hair and body, rinsing away the heaviness clinging to her. By the time she stepped out, she felt a little lighter.

Ella had left clothes on the chair days ago - just in case she was ready. Janey pulled on the soft leggings and baggy t-shirt, then tugged the cosy purple sweatshirt over her head, pulling the hood up and wrapping her arms around herself. She sank into its warmth.

Chapter 53

After her shower, feeling refreshed but with a restless energy beginning to stir inside of her, Janey called Ella into her room. Ella came in and settled on the wee chair by the window, wondering why she'd been summoned.

Janey sat up straight on the bed, trying to act as if it were just another day. Her eyes and nose still had a faint greenish tinge and a trace of swelling, but she looked remarkably better compared to the state she'd been in only days ago.

But they both knew – this wasn't just another day.

Janey took a deep breath and began explaining her immediate plans for the future. Ella listened, nodding in the right places, but something felt off. She didn't want to wrap Janey in cotton wool and keep her tucked away in Miss Powell's house forever – but neither did she want her heading back to Rab's flat, with its shadow of violence and the lure of drugs.

Janey said she was grateful for being able to stay a few days, but now it was time to move on.

'Okay,' said Ella. 'Where will you go? I know Mum will be happy to have you back. You don't have to tell her the full story if you're not ready.'

Janey shifted uncomfortably, eyes flicking away. She said she'd arranged to stay with her friend Becky in Leith.

Ella knew instantly she was lying. Janey couldn't meet her gaze, and since she didn't have her mobile, there was no obvious way she'd contacted Becky. As far as Ella knew, she hadn't touched the house phone in Miss Powell's living room, and she certainly hadn't borrowed Ella's.

Then came the scratching – Janey's nails dragging over her arms and legs.

Ella had seen withdrawal before. She recognised the restless agitation, the need building under the skin.

Janey thought her sister knew nothing about the drugs, but Ella had been watching her decline for over a year - the weight loss, the eyes that were either unnaturally wide or pin-sharp, the erratic swings from manic to flat.

Ella herself had dabbled in recreational and prescription drugs when she was younger, but after a close friend overdosed and nearly died - ending up in a psychiatric ward - she'd stopped instantly. That experience had burned the warning signs into her memory.

She didn't challenge Janey outright. Accusing her of lying and planning to run straight back to Rab's flat would only shut her down.

Ella could take the easy route - send her away with homeopathic pills, tinctures, and teas, pretending to believe her promise to stay with Becky. That way, she could wash her hands of it, tell herself she'd done her bit.

But she loved her sister too much for that. Janey was trapped in a self-destructive cycle, and Ella couldn't just let her walk straight back into it without trying to break it.

Janey, for her part, thought she was convincing. She was certain Ella believed her story. All she really wanted was to get back to the flat, forgive Rab for now, roll a fat joint, pop a couple of downers, and maybe - tomorrow - think about finding a new place. It wasn't the wisest plan, but it was the one that would get her through the next few days. She told herself she'd really try to move on... though deep down she wasn't sure she could.

The one thing Janey had expected from Ella was a fight - some pushback, a lecture about abuse or drugs or the dangers of going back. But Ella just nodded.

In reality, Ella's mind was turning. She needed a plan, something to shake Janey out of her complicity.

Yesterday, she'd suggested a professional counsellor, and Janey had brushed it off with a 'maybe later.' Ella knew she'd never make that appointment on her own.

What Janey needed was a jolt - a shock that would break through her haze.

Ella's thoughts drifted to the golden mirror. The lessons she'd learned when she stepped through to other times and places had changed her profoundly.

She made up her mind. She would take Janey through. But not to the grand delights of Jenners on Princes Street or any charming past scene. No - she would take her to the workhouse at Craiglockhart. Show her the life of women who had no choices, no escape.

It would be a brutal contrast to Janey's modern freedom - a mirror not of gold, but of stark reality.

Ella looked at her sister, quietly confident she'd found the plan that might finally break the cycle.

Chapter 54

Ella took a deep breath, weighing her words carefully, wondering how to draw Janey in without revealing everything too soon.

'Okay,' said Ella, 'I understand you want to go - but before you leave, I want to show you something... or should I say somewhere.'

Janey's shoulders stiffened. She wasn't in the mood for detours. 'I dunno that I want to go anywhere,' she muttered, sliding into a sulky resistance at the thought of her plans being interfered with. 'It won't take long. We don't even have to go very far,' said Ella. A mysterious note crept into her voice. 'Well... not in the first instance,' she added mysteriously.

'I'm not in the mood to go anywhere or meet anyone.' Janey's suspicion flared - she had a feeling Ella might have arranged a meeting with a counsellor or therapist. She wasn't about to sit in front of some stranger talking about her life.

'I think I'll just head out and stick to my plan,' Janey said, stubbornness in full force as she got up from the bed, as if to leave right then. 'I just need to get on with my life.'

'Honestly, it won't take that long, Janey. And believe me - you've never experienced anything like this before.' Ella leaned forward slightly. 'I wasn't going to share this with you - possibly ever - what I've discovered, the places I've been... without even leaving this building.'

She let her voice drop, adding just enough mystery to hook her. 'The people I've met... the things I've seen... these past few months.' She paused, watching Janey closely. Janey, despite herself, started to look intrigued. She sat back down, though her eyes still narrowed with suspicion. She knew her sister

CHAPTER 54

was trying to delay her departure, but she couldn't help being drawn in.

'You know those times when you thought I was out - and Miss Powell thought I might be in the attic - but despite looking for me, I was nowhere to be found?' Ella asked. 'Well... I was in the attic. But behind the golden mirrored door.' Janey stared. Then shook her head.

'Aye right, so you were sitting in the attic in a cupboard all that time? Ella, I know you love a story, but this is daft. I can see you want to delay me leaving, but it's not going to work.' Ella's face fell, the hurt showing. Janey noticed - and it made her feel bad - Ella had done so much for her. So she told Ella how much she appreciated everything Ella had done for her: the teas and tinctures, the healing care, the patience... and Miss Powell's generosity in giving her the time and space to recover in such a beautiful home.

'This is different, Janey,' Ella said, her tone low but certain. 'I've found a portal to another world - one that takes me back in time.'

Janey blinked, then gave her sister a look usually reserved for people talking about UFO sightings. Had Ella been taking mushrooms or something? Still... the idea of some mind-bending trip wasn't unappealing. If her straight-laced sister was offering to take her on some wild, psychedelic journey, she was suddenly interested.

'Go on then,' Janey said with a smirk. 'Tell me what you want to do with me. I can't wait to hear this.'

'There's no way it's what you're thinking,' Ella replied, half-smiling at the glint in her sister's eye. She could imagine exactly where Janey's mind had gone.

Ella knew she had no choice now - the only way forward was to tell Janey the truth about the time-travelling portal behind the golden mirror.

Chapter 55

Over the next hour, Ella wove the story of discovering the space behind the golden mirror and travelling back in time, leaving nothing out. She told her sister about the people she had met, the places she had gone, and the strange wonder of seeing the house, the asylum, and the city over a hundred years ago.

Janey had not been expecting this. Part of her was carried along by Ella's vivid descriptions, but another part thought, *How is any of this possible?* Although Ella was a storyteller, Janey knew she wasn't a liar. Was it really possible she had found a time-travelling portal?

'So,' said Ella, bringing her back, 'are you willing to come through and see how people lived in the past?'

As much as Janey wanted to move on with her life, the prospect intrigued her. She decided she'd go, though she had no idea Ella's real plan was to shock her into changing her path by showing her the darker side of old Edinburgh and how few choices women had back then. Ella wasn't sure if it would work; she just knew she couldn't let Janey go back to Rab.

'Aye, all right,' agreed Janey. 'When are we going?'

Ella felt both relief and nerves. She had no idea what would happen taking someone else through the mirror. Still, she decided to cast a protection circle once they were inside the cupboard.

'Right now.' Ella jumped to her feet and left her room before either of them could change their mind.

Janey followed her up the attic stairs, unimpressed by the dusty trunks and boxes. But when her eyes landed on the golden mirror, her expression

CHAPTER 55

softened.

'Wow. That's a magical-looking mirror.'

'It is,' said Ella, delighted by her reaction. 'It's my portal to another world. Come with me - play along, relax, enjoy the experience.'

Janey knew her sister was into witchy poo and new age things - rituals, sacred circles, herbal medicine - none of which had ever really interested her. Still, she was always up for trying something new.

Ella unlocked the golden mirror's door and stepped inside, beckoning her to follow.

'The first thing I want to do is put a circle of protection around us. Turn to face me.'

It was awkward in the tight space, but Janey obeyed. Ella guided her through deep breaths, then spoke softly:

'Imagine a white light above our heads, swirling down around us like a cloak until it reaches our feet, wrapping us in a thick, protective shield. This light will keep us safe on our journey.'

By the end, Janey felt oddly calm, able to picture the white glow holding them.

'Now,' Ella said, 'turn again. We're going to spin three times clockwise together. You might feel the world spin around you - but don't worry. Once we step back into the attic, we'll be invisible. Stick with me. Promise you won't float off.'

'Yeah, whatever,' Janey said with a smirk - until she saw how serious Ella's face was. 'Okay. I promise.'

They spun around together. On the third turn, the cupboard walls seemed to melt away. 'Whoa!' Janey cried, grabbing Ella. 'What the hell is happening?' It was like flying through a starry void. Her jaw tingled, her vision filled with blackness though her eyes felt wide open. The sensation was unsettling - like the first seconds of a bad trip.

Ella's arms tightened around her. 'Shhh. You're safe. You're with me.' Ella herself wasn't entirely sure they were safe; she'd never brought anyone with her before. But she steadied her thoughts, fixed her mind on their destination, and pushed her energy forward. At last, the spinning stopped. 'Janey - can you hear me?'

'Yes. What just happened?' Asked Janey, her voice trembling.

'If it worked, we're still in the same place… only now it's over a hundred years ago. Can you feel my energy?'

'I can… but I can't see you. I can't even see myself.'

'That's okay. Pretend you've taken the most incredible pill – one that makes your body disappear and lets you float through another time. Just stay with me.' Janey took a breath and agreed.

Shapes began to emerge. They were in the attic, but it had changed. Now it was filled with old toys, a dollhouse, rails of gowns and dresses.

'Ooh, look at those clothes!' Janey gasped, drifting closer.

'There's more to see. Stay with me.' This time, Janey didn't argue. She felt safer close to Ella. Together, they floated down the stairs into the old house, which looked even more quaint than the last time Ella had visited. The hall was empty.

'Hold on,' Ella said. 'We're going outside.'

Chapter 56

The sisters floated through the front door. Ella hesitated by the row of coats and hats, wondering if they should make themselves visible by putting on clothes. She decided against it – best to stay unseen.

'Wait a minute,' Janey gasped. 'I recognise this place. Oh my goodness, this is Miss Powell's house, but...!' She couldn't finish; she was too overwhelmed.

'Yes,' Ella said gently, finishing for her. 'It is – but maybe a hundred years ago or more. The same... yet very, very different.' She gave Janey a moment to take it in. 'Stick with me, Janey. There's so much to see.' They floated high above the trees, heading south – the opposite direction Ella usually took. The treetops stretched below them like a vast green sea.

Janey let out a breath she hadn't realised she'd been holding. Her heart raced with disbelief and excitement. *This is real*, she thought, *I'm floating.* A laugh bubbled up, half delight, half fear. *This is incredible.* The world felt bigger, more alive. For the first time in a long while, she felt like anything was possible.

They drifted over rooftops until the city's poorhouse came into view.

Ella knew it well. In her own time, the grim Gothic building had been transformed into exclusive apartments in the 1980s. She had walked the grounds often, wondering about its past. The first time she'd asked Miss Powell about it, her eyes had lit with the promise of a story.

'Are you still interested in knowing about those Gothic buildings with the tower up the road?' Miss Powell had asked one afternoon, teacup in hand.

'Yes,' Ella had said, leaning forward.

'Well,' Miss Powell began, 'it started life in the Victorian era as a poorhouse

- the last refuge for those with nowhere else to go. Life there was grim. Men, women, and children were separated, then split again by 'class.' The healthy worked seven days a week for their keep - men as labourers, tailors, carpenters, shoemakers, farmhands; women and children in the kitchens, scrubbing floors, or in the dreaded laundry. And always under strict, harsh rules.'

She had gone on to describe how the poorhouse also housed 160 'insane' inmates in their mini asylum area and could hold over a thousand more in the other parts of the building. It was designed to run on a skeleton staff; it relied on wardens patrolling endless corridors, keeping people subdued with the threat of corporal punishment or the asylum. Abuse between inmates was rife; no one dared speak out.

'By the 1920s,' Miss Powell had said, 'the place had fallen under heartless masters and matrons. Poorhouses were made as unpleasant as possible so folk would rather risk the streets.'

Ella had shivered. 'I didn't know they were such cruel places.'

'Aye, lass. It's important to remember, so we never go back.'

Miss Powell's tale had continued through the years - the poorhouse turned into a home for the elderly in the mid-20th century, then sold off under Thatcher and renovated into luxury flats.

'Every building has its secrets, my dear,' Miss Powell had said, smiling over her tea. 'You just have to listen.'

Now, in the past, Ella and Janey hovered above that same poorhouse - but the lawns were bare, the windows unpolished, and the air heavy with a sense of watchful silence. 'Ready to go in?' Ella asked quietly. Janey swallowed. 'I... think so.'

Chapter 57

As Ella and Janey floated down to the front of the poorhouse, Ella was glad that she had recently learned so much of its history from Miss Powell.

It was a large, imposing building with a clock tower of over a hundred feet. The surrounding area looked like a working farm with a pen with pigs, cows in a field and a large hen house.

Many men were working around the grounds, wearing stripy work uniforms, immediately identifying them as inmates of the poorhouse. Ella floated through the main door with Janey not far behind.

'Oh my god, what a depressing place this is. What is it?' asked Janey.

'This is the Edinburgh poorhouse,' replied Ella. 'Miss Powell told me loads about the history of this place just a couple of weeks ago. This is where you had to go when you had no choices in life, destitute and had nowhere else to go.'

They floated through another door and found themselves in a cold, windowless room. They soon realised they were in the area where new inmates were checked into the poorhouse.

The building was cold and dark, smelling of dampness and unclean bodies, as well as rotten food. The dark and the smell of the poorhouse clung around the sisters. They felt the dense atmosphere close in around them, and they found comfort knowing each other was there.

They looked around them. In the room was a large, stern-looking woman dressed in a black dress, white apron and white cap, and two big men in stripy inmate clothes. It was plain to see she was in charge and probably the matron or supervisor of the poorhouse.

'Right,' said the matron to her two workers, 'we have at least five new inmates that need to be processed this morning. I've got a very busy morning, so let's get to it.' She had a raspy, rough voice with a thick Scottish accent. The sisters shuddered at the thought of being under her 'care'.

The two men appeared to be taking on the role of assistant wardens. They disappeared into the outer room and came back with a fragile-looking, youngish woman, almost carrying her between them.

One of the wardens was pressing himself close to the new inmate and one warden had his hand buried deep into her rag-like clothes around her backside. Ella could see he was having a quick feel of her. The new inmate gave him a look as if she wanted to kick him. 'Get your hand off my arse,' said the young woman.

'Don't you dare talk like that,' snapped the matron at the poor woman. 'You are here at the mercy of the poorhouse committee, and you will show your gratitude. Any cheek or improper behaviour from you, and believe me, you'll be punished - or thrown right back into the slum you came from.'

The matron sounded harsh and cruel. The young woman looked utterly terrified, wondering what she had done by walking in through the door of the poorhouse, but terrifying as the matron was, the man she had been living with would not let her leave and threatened to kill her if she did, and this was the only place she could think of to go.

She was dressed in rags and had severe bruises around her eyes and a missing front tooth that looked like it had been lost recently. There was dried blood around her mouth and nose.

The woman looked unhappy and hungry, yet still had a spark of life in her eyes that said not all was lost.

One of the wardens spoke up. 'Paperwork has been done, Matron. This is Morag Campbell, who thinks she is about 21 years old, has no birth certificate and says she doesn't know who her mam or father is. She is an unmarried woman who has been living with a man. She claims that if she stays with him, he may kill her next time,' under his breath he continued, 'She looks to me like she deserved whatever she got, she seems a bit of a wildcat.'

'You are not here to give your opinions, warden. Just do your job and shut

CHAPTER 57

up,' said the matron.

She looked at the entry form and then looked scornfully at the woman.

'She doesn't have any family to take her in and says she hasn't eaten for three days,' confirmed the other warden.

The matron puffed herself up with self-importance and began to lecture her. 'This is a poorhouse, not a whore house. You will work every day, and in return, you will get fed every day. There are rules and regulations that you will be informed about in good time. If you break any of these rules, you will be discharged from here immediately and have to leave. In the meantime, strip off your clothes. Your rags will be steamed and put away. You will get them back when you are discharged, along with any of your other possessions.'

The woman looked at the matron and then the two wardens. 'What, you want me to strip here, now?'

'Get on with it, woman. You haven't got anything that we haven't seen before or something that you haven't shown before, by the sounds of your sluttish life. There is a bath next door that I will supervise. We need to make sure you have no lice and are cleaned properly. You will get a bath once a week unless you are told you are exempt by the medical officer. Get to it, or I'll take the strap to you, or you can go back to the slum that you just left.'

The poor woman began to take off her apron and dress. The material was so thin that it could almost be seen through. It had rips and tears in it, and it looked like it was held together by muck and grime. She shamefully removed her filthy undergarments and stood there naked.

She was so thin that her ribs and hipbones stuck out. Her body was covered with a variety of bruises, in all different sizes and colours, and she had a huge purple bruise on her chest.

She stood there, trying to cover herself with her rake-thin arms, and was pushed through to the other room by the wardens.

The sisters followed through and watched as the woman was pushed towards the tin bath. Ella and Janey watched the steam rising from the tin bath and could see how hot the water was.

The woman put her foot into the bath and whimpered at the feeling of the burning water on her skin. 'We haven't got all day. Get yourself in there,' said one of the wardens.

She slowly submerged herself into the water, making small yelping noises as she was forced into the boiling hot water. One of the wardens had a brush that he covered in some kind of carbolic soap and began to scrub her so hard that she screamed again. They pushed her head under the water and gave her some soap to scrub into her hair and rinse off.

She was then told to stand up and was scrubbed with the brush again from head to toe. She was told to open her legs, and one of the wardens took far too much time using a cloth to clean between her legs with a leery look on his face. The whole process was humiliating and painful to look at.

At the end of the ordeal, she was ordered out and given a thin piece of rag to dry herself as best she could and on the floor was a pile of clothes she was told to get into.

The clothes looked like they were made from scratchy, harsh material and were ill-fitting for the young woman. She was given undergarments, a vest, a heavy sack-like dress, an apron, a shawl, a cap and boots that she looked like she had to squeeze her feet into.

She immediately looked twenty years older in the ill-fitting poorhouse uniform. She hung her head, and when she looked back up, Ella could see that the spark in her eyes that had been there when she first arrived had gone.

The matron ordered the wardens to put her into the holding room because other unfortunate individuals were waiting to be processed. They frogmarched the young woman out of the room.

Ella could feel Janey's sadness and anger toward this woman.

'Is this woman here because she has nowhere else to go and doesn't want to get beaten up by her violent partner?' asked Janey.

'Yes,' said Ella, knowing that Janey was upset and couldn't believe what she was seeing.

'The poor woman.' Janey was almost crying for this poor creature.

The Matron returned to the room and demanded that the next case be brought in. The wardens brought in a thin older woman and two tiny, skinny children, dressed in rags and all looking terrified.

'I can't bear to watch this process again. Can we get out of here?' said Janey.

CHAPTER 57

They seeped their energy out of the door and into the main hall, leaving the poor family to the wrath of the matron and the wardens.

Chapter 58

The sisters found themselves in the centre of the poorhouse. As Miss Powell had described, it had a very long, straight corridor connecting the West and East Wings.

They floated along until they reached a dormitory just off the main corridor. Inside were at least thirty beds, lined up in two neat but lifeless rows beneath a single, grimy window. The air was thick and sour with the stench of urine, faeces, and the unwashed bodies of those who had no means to clean themselves.

The bed frames were cold iron, the thin mattresses stuffed with straw. Each bed had a single, threadbare blanket and a box underneath - perhaps all the space a person had for their possessions. Rats scurried along the backs of the cots, pausing to gnaw at crumbs.

Janey's voice trembled. 'This is horrible... these poor people.' Her words were soaked in both disgust and sympathy. They left the stench behind and floated down the corridor into the other wing. Ella could tell Janey had almost had enough.

Janey was freaked out. When Ella had described her time-travelling, it had sounded magical and exciting - not dark, oppressive, and hopeless. She wanted out. She couldn't believe people had lived like this, and the reality was pressing down on her chest like a weight.

But Ella wasn't ready to leave. Miss Powell's stories had never hinted at this level of detail, and now that she was here, she wanted to see more.

'Stick with me - we'll be okay,' Ella assured her.

Reluctant but unwilling to be alone, Janey followed her into a large,

CHAPTER 58

sweltering room – the laundry.

At least a hundred women and children stood with arms deep in steaming water, scrubbing sheets, towels, and clothes. The heat was suffocating. Sweat trickled down the faces of the women, their hair plastered to their foreheads. They wore the same coarse, heavy uniforms the sisters had seen issued to a newly arrived inmate.

As they floated closer, they saw fine linens, crisp shirts, and embroidered gowns pass through the wash. These clothes clearly belonged to the wealthy – it looked like the poorhouse inmates were laundering for Edinburgh's elite.

Above the slosh of water and the hiss of steam, a bell clanged, sharp and metallic. The workers set down their tools and moved to another part of the building.

The sisters followed into a huge, damp hall with high ceilings and two long windows letting in grey light. Rows of rough wooden tables stretched the length of the room. Men sat on one side, women and children on the other. On the stone wall above them hung a wooden plaque: GOD IS GOOD.

Huge pots of gruel stood at the head table, each inmate receiving a single ladle dumped into their bowl. The slop was grey, lumpy, and unappealing. Janey's eyes brimmed. 'It's like they're being punished for being poor.'

The hopelessness in the room was palpable – a heavy, suffocating presence clung to the sisters like a damp cloth. Ella had planned to show Janey the slums of old Edinburgh next, but even she had had enough.

'I hear you,' Ella said quietly. 'We've seen enough. Let's go home.'

'Thank goodness, ' Janey breathed.

They floated up through the ceiling, over the poorhouse, and back towards the familiar shape of Miss Powell's corner house. Through the front door, up to the attic, past trunks and boxes, and straight to the golden mirror.

'Hold on to me,' Ella instructed.

They spun three times anti-clockwise. The world swirled dizzily, then stilled.

They stepped back into Miss Powell's attic, safe and sound.

Ella let out a quiet sigh of relief. She would never tell Janey how much she'd worried they might not make it back.

Chapter 59

Janey stepped out of the attic and looked around, scanning the familiar shadows and sloping beams of Miss Powell's attic just to be sure they were back. She turned to Ella, eyes wide.

'What the hell was that? That wasn't very nice and not magical at all. You made it sound amazing when you told me about your time-travelling tunnel. That was the worst experience of my life.' Janey looked drained, her face tight with both anger and exhaustion.

Ella took Janey by the hand and led her downstairs into her bedroom, bracing herself for the barrage of questions that was sure to come. Janey slumped onto the sofa, her gaze fixed on Ella, demanding answers without saying another word.

'Look, I know that was a weird experience, but it was real. I can't explain how it happens - it just does.' Ella took a deep breath. 'What you just experienced was Edinburgh about a hundred years ago, maybe even further back. I don't know why I can do it or how the magic of the mirror works... I just know that it does.'

She studied her sister. 'Janey, you look exhausted. Maybe you should sleep a little before you make any decisions or go anywhere.' The pallor of Janey's skin made the green and yellow bruises on her face stand out even more starkly.

Janey sat there in silence, still processing. 'That poor woman in the poorhouse... I didn't know or even imagine people ever lived like that.' Her voice cracked as the image returned - the bruised young woman, spirit broken, starving, with nowhere to go.

CHAPTER 59

She began to cry - at first for the woman in the poorhouse, and then, as something broke open inside her, for herself. Soon her quiet tears became heavy sobs. She hadn't cried since Rab's attack, keeping her emotions locked away. Now the floodgates opened, and she let the sobs spill out.

Ella moved closer, scooping Janey into her arms. 'It's okay, Janey. Things have changed now. People - especially women - have so much more control and choice in their lives these days.'

Ella held her sister, wanting desperately for her to see the choices she still had, but knowing this was not the moment for advice or lectures. She could only hope the experience would plant a seed in Janey's mind. The rest was up to her.

'My head is so full right now. I think I'll go to sleep for a bit before I go,' Janey murmured. 'Do you think Miss Powell will mind?' Janey looked at Ella, pleading with her eyes. 'I'm sure she won't mind at all. Lie down - there's no rush.'

Janey left the bedroom with slow, heavy steps and made her way to the spare room. She felt safe there. Pulling the blankets around her, she sank into the bed, her limbs weighted with exhaustion. Images of the poorhouse drifted through her mind - the young woman forced to surrender her liberty and freedom, simply because she was poor.

Janey's heart ached for her. How awful to live in a world with no choices and such cruelty. Deep down, she knew there were still people in the world today who had few choices. But, she told herself, she wasn't one of them. Eventually, she slipped into a deep, dreamless sleep.

Ella, meanwhile, sat in her room, unsettled. That trip back in time had been the most harrowing yet. She was still unsure whether she should have taken Janey at all. Janey could be unpredictable - and what if she told someone what lay behind the golden mirror?

Chapter 60

Janey woke up a few hours later, her mind clearer, her thoughts sharper. The mystery of what had happened behind that golden mirror still hung in the air. Was it a dream? A hallucination?

Did she really visit a poorhouse from over a hundred years ago? She remembered Ella giving her a cup of herbal tea that morning. Could there have been something in it that sent her spinning into another world?

Ella could spin an amazing story when she wanted to, but what Janey had felt that morning was on a completely different level. Unsure of what she had experienced, she figured that maybe trying to make sense of it all wasn't what she needed right now.

Sometimes, Janey thought, *things happen in life and you just have to go along with them - take the lessons and move on.* She caught herself thinking that and almost laughed. 'Did I just say that?' It was exactly the kind of thing Ella would say. Maybe they were more alike than she realised.

She got up and dressed, then stood in front of the mirror. Until now, every time she looked at herself she'd seen only weakness - the girl who stayed, the girl who put up with it. But now... now she felt different.

When she looked at her reflection and the bruises, she felt anger - hot, sharp - not at herself, but at her so-called boyfriend. Who the hell did he think he was to do that to her?

She knew then she would never go back to him. She knew she deserved better, and above all, she knew she had choices. It was like someone had flipped a switch inside her.

This was the most hopeful she had felt in a long time. Whatever had

CHAPTER 60

happened that morning had cracked something open deep inside – an undeniable awareness of how lucky she was to live in a time when women had choices. Everything clicked into place. She knew exactly what she wanted – and needed – to do. For the first time in what felt like forever, she was back in control of her life.

She also knew that, while many of her friends would happily let her crash on their sofas, most of them lived for late nights, heavy drinking, and endless clubbing – and that life no longer appealed. She needed time away from drinking, drugs and clubs to heal and think about her future.

She knew she couldn't stay at Miss Powell's forever. Going home to her mum suddenly felt like a safe harbour – somewhere to stop, breathe, and decide her next steps.

Ella's mobile was on the hall table, and Janey was sure she wouldn't mind her using it. She called her mum, who was surprised to hear Janey's voice instead of Ella's. As they spoke, her mum quickly realised Janey needed help.

Janey explained that she and Rab had split up and asked if she could come home for a few weeks until she sorted herself out. She left out the worst of it – now wasn't the time to burden her mum with all her pain.

Her mum was secretly delighted about the breakup. She had only met Rab once, but that had been enough to decide she didn't like or trust him. She didn't ask many questions – just said, 'Yes, of course, come home for as long as you need.'

Their adopted mum loved them as if they were her own flesh and blood, and it warmed her heart to know Janey still considered her house *home*.

Janey packed what little she had with her and found Ella in the living room with Miss Powell. 'Ella, I'm not sure what happened this morning, but I'm going to put it down to your incredible storytelling powers.'

Ella smiled. 'I think that's the best way to look at it – and not look for any more explanations.' Ella knew then that her secret of the golden mirror was safe.

Janey turned to Miss Powell. 'I can't thank you enough for letting me stay here. I'm sorry to have brought trouble to your door, but this has been an amazing place to begin healing and sorting my head out.' Miss Powell smiled, listening without interrupting.

Then Janey faced Ella. 'I've called Mum, and I'm going to go back there for a wee while until I find somewhere else to live. I am not going back to that,' she stopped herself, glancing at Miss Powell, 'man's flat again. Not by myself, anyway.'

Ella listened, astonished. This was a different Janey from the one she'd spoken to that morning.

'Sounds like a great plan. Do you want to give me your key, and I'll ask Scott to take me down so we can pack your stuff and bring it to you?'

Janey considered it. 'I need closure on this chapter. I'll go down and pack my stuff myself, but I promise I won't go alone - and I'd love your help when I do.' Ella's heart lifted. Janey, asking for help - something really had shifted. Before their trip that morning, Janey had been ready to walk straight back into the same mess, no matter what she'd told Ella.

'I'm actually looking forward to going back to Mum's for a little while,' Janey said - and this time, she meant it. 'I'll call you tomorrow and we'll sort a time to clear your flat, ' Ella replied, smiling. She was just happy to hear her sister being honest with herself for the first time in a very long time.

Chapter 61

Ella sat quietly in the front room with Miss Powell. The house felt calmer now, the air lighter, after the past few stormy days.

When Janey left, she carried a different air about her - not the loud confidence of an exhibitionist and girl-about-town, but the quiet, steady confidence of a woman who had taken back control of her life.

She'd left with hugs and words of gratitude for them both, promising to be in touch when she was stronger so they could arrange a time to pick up her belongings from her ex-boyfriend - a term she now used freely for Rab.

Ella was sure Janey would be heading straight to Mum's house, not to that dark, dingy basement flat she'd once shared with that creep. Something in Janey had changed since their visit through the golden mirror.

Ella thought back to their trip into the past. She hadn't known what would happen when she took Janey through. She realised she had taken an enormous chance and was grateful they'd both returned safely - and that the experience had left Janey stronger.

The more Ella reflected, the more certain she was that the place they'd visited had felt different from her previous journeys - harsher, bleaker, with conditions that almost seemed Victorian. Had she travelled further back in time than usual? She couldn't be sure, and maybe she never would be.

If that was the case, then she didn't have any control over when she arrived - and that made it unpredictable... and exciting.

She became aware that Miss Powell was speaking to her.

'Sorry, Miss Powell, I was in a bit of a daydream. What did you say?'

'I said, make sure it's not just you and Janey that go down to that beast's house when you collect her things. I'm sure Scott would be happy to help. You know, there's more to that boy than meets the eye. You know, underneath that happy-go-lucky exterior of his is a streetwise man who's seen things that would make you and me shudder.'

'Really?' said Ella, intrigued. 'I know he's from a rough part of town, and he's done well for himself with his own business and flat, but I don't know much else. Remind me - how do you know each other?'

'We used to volunteer for the same organisation in Pilton,' Miss Powell said. 'His story isn't mine to tell, but I can tell you this: I trust that boy as much as if he were my own. He's a good lad, had a hard start in life through no fault of his own. As you get older, you learn to listen to your intuition about people - not judge them for where they came from or what they've done.'

'I try to do that. I think I'm getting better,' said Ella. Especially on her time travel adventures, she thought. 'I might potter about in the attic for a while, or maybe go out - that is, if you don't need me here.'

'No, I have everything I need, lass. Just be careful not to spend too much time living in the past when there's so much to learn in the present,' Miss Powell said wisely.

Does she know more than she's letting on? Ella wondered. *Nah - she's just being wise.*

'I will,' Ella promised, already feeling the pull to step through the mirror again.

Her thoughts drifted to Scott. He had been cool and understanding around Janey, but she'd sensed his underlying anger and disgust at Rab for what he'd done to her.

He had told Ella he'd be happy to go down to the flat, sort Rab out, and retrieve Janey's belongings. Ella wasn't entirely sure what he meant by *sorting Rab out*, but she had a fair idea. She told him she didn't believe in fighting violence with violence - if they did that, they'd be no better than him.

Scott thought about it, then nodded in agreement. She explained that Janey had decided to leave Rab for good, and they would be grateful for his presence when the time came to collect her things - but it might not be for a week or

CHAPTER 61

two.

Scott didn't hesitate. 'I'm there for you, Ella. Don't put yourself in danger for a moment - I'll come with you,' he said.

His words felt like an invisible hug - warm, steady, and sincere. Ella believed him, and it was good to know they had him on their side.

Chapter 62

Scott had been shaken by the state of Janey when he caught a glimpse of her at Miss Powell's house a couple of days after she arrived. She had stepped out into the back garden for some fresh air, and when she turned, he saw her swollen, bruised face. The fight in her eyes was gone.

She looked like a shadow of her former self. He gave her a quick nod, not wanting to stare, and got back to his work. Ella had told him what had happened, but seeing the injuries in person hit differently.

He felt a rush of disgust that a so-called man had done this to his girlfriend. Years ago, the old Scott would have picked up a steel bar and gone looking for him, but Scott wasn't that man anymore.

After talking with Ella about violence and her belief that fighting wasn't the way forward, he realised he felt the same deep down. He had to ignore his knee-jerk urge to beat Rab to a pulp.

Someone like Rab would probably expect someone to come after him with fists - maybe even welcome the challenge. Worse, he might think he'd get away with it.

The more Scott thought about it, the more he concluded Rab deserved a far deeper hurt than a black eye that would fade in a few days. If he wanted to make an impact, it had to be something that would sting his pride and crack the image he valued most. As far as Scott was concerned, Rab wasn't a man at all - just a bully and a coward.

Scott wanted to do something that would stick with him - a slow burn, the kind of blow that would make him think twice before raising a hand to a woman, or anyone weaker than him, ever again. Psychological warfare, he

CHAPTER 62

decided, was exactly what Rab deserved.

He couldn't stop thinking about it. When he got home, he cracked open a beer, sat back, and let his mind sift through what he knew about Rab.

Scott only knew him from a distance. They'd drunk in some of the same pubs and clubs, where Rab and his brother always made sure they were the loudest in the room. Everyone knew Rab as a bully and a small-time drug dealer.

He was a dock worker, part of a tough crowd, and liked to flash a wedge of cash around town. The designer (knock-off) clothes, the flashy watch, the big car - it was all part of the act. To him, appearances were currency.

For as long as Scott had known him, Rab always had a good-looking woman on his arm and the swagger to match. He also had a reputation for taking cocaine and speed on his nights out, Valium the next day, and, according to rumours, even heroin when he needed to come down after a heavy weekend.

He was, as Scott saw it, a functioning addict who kept up appearances - smart clothes, steady job, nights out in the city - all the while propped up by him and his brother's dealing and their shared willingness to use violence to keep people in line.

To a man like Rab, reputation was everything. Scott just needed the right way to destroy it - to strip away the false glamour and show him for what he really was.

Ella had taken photos of all Janey's injuries the night she arrived, in case she later decided to press charges. When Scott asked if he could use them to get back at Rab, Janey's first answer was no. She wanted to handle it her way.

But yesterday, Ella called to say Janey had changed her mind. She knew she'd done nothing wrong, and if Scott wanted to use the photos to teach Rab a lesson, she was fine with it.

Scott got to work. On his laptop, he made a series of posters - photos of Janey's bruises alongside one pulled from Rab's public Facebook page. This wasn't going to be random payback. It would be timed, co-ordinated, and delivered from every angle, hitting Rab so hard and so fast he'd feel ambushed from all directions.

Chapter 63

Rab Jackson, Janey's ex-boyfriend, had no idea what was coming. He was going about his life as usual.

As was his routine, he got ready for work and strutted out of his flat. Morning shift today meant a bacon roll and coffee at his usual café before heading to the docks.

It had been over a week since his stupid girlfriend, Janey had, in his mind, *got what she deserved.* She still hadn't come back - but she would. They always did. In his head, she loved his lifestyle, the drugs, and him too much to stay away. He was already picturing her coming back, tail between her legs, begging to return.

As he approached the café, the usual locals were outside, smoking and sipping coffee. Normally, they'd greet him, maybe banter a bit. Not today. This time, when they saw him, they laughed and turned their backs. He thought he heard one of the guys mutter, '*Fuck off back to the gutter, ya wife-beater.*'

Nah, he thought, *I'm hearing things.* He put a charming smile on his face for the cute girl who worked behind the counter, that he always flirted with.

She turned to greet him, a smile in place for the next customer - until she saw him. Her smile dropped instantly.

'You can just fuck off, you scabby wife-beater. You're not welcome here,' she snapped, pointing at a poster on the wall. 'Tell him, Dave.' Dave, the manager, stepped forward. 'You heard her. Get out - and dinnae come back.' Rab's gut tightened. What the hell was going on? He turned to where she'd pointed.

CHAPTER 63

There it was. A poster of him, growling at the camera - a shot he remembered because Janey had taken it after a long, drug-fueled night when he'd been in a foul mood. Beside it were pictures of Janey... only barely recognisable. Blackened eyes. Blood-matted hair. Swollen nose. Her face was a mess of snot, blood, and bruises.

Beneath the photo, it read:

Rab Jackson, Leith Walk. Works at the Docks. WOMAN BEATER AND BULLY.

His stomach lurched. *That bitch.* As he left, the cute girl's glare burned into his back. Outside, an old man spat at him and hissed, 'Scumbag.'

Then he saw them - posters plastered on lamp posts, bins, bus stops. His rage built as he tore each one down. He told himself it was nothing. He'd knocked her about because he'd been in a bad mood, and she'd been in the wrong place at the wrong time. He'd done it before - not just to her. *What's the big deal?*

He pulled out his phone to distract himself. Bad idea. His face was everywhere on his Facebook pages. Forty-eight shares of the poster already. Comments stacked up, each one nastier than the last. His page had become a firing squad - for him.

And it wasn't guilt that he felt now - it was the embarrassment of the photos! Also, his reputation, his life, was unravelling. The sheer unfairness of it made his blood boil.

He shoved the phone away and jumped on a bus to work, telling himself the lads at the docks wouldn't care. But as soon as he stepped off, he saw more posters. Even the security guys sneered, 'Wife-beater.'

Inside the yard, one of his mates shouted, 'Shottie! Here comes the woman-beating wanker!' The whole yard jeered. His shift manager - a big man known for being fair but firm - called him into the office. On the desk lay the poster.

'You scumbag,' the manager said coldly, as soon as the door closed. 'Most of us have met Janey. She's a cracking lass. The lads don't want to work beside you, and we have a big contract on - it's in my best interests to keep them happy! You are going to take two months' unpaid leave - starting now. This isn't optional.'

Rab glanced outside. The mob was still jeering. He'd been part of that mob before, targeting others. Now the rules of the docks – like prison – applied to him. There were lines you didn't cross, and he'd crossed one. He signed the paper. Walked out. Got spat on again.

By the time he reached his flat, tearing down posters as he went, he just wanted whisky, weed, and the world shut out.

No such luck. His front door was wide open. Inside stood Janey and standing behind her – Scott and Ella. 'We're here to collect my stuff,' Janey said.

Scott's presence said, without words: *Don't try anything.* Bags and suitcases were moved to the stairwell. Janey did one last sweep, then stood in front of him, shoulders square.

'You are a real scumbag,' she said. 'I can't believe it took me so long to leave. I hope every time you look in the mirror, you remember me and what you did. You are nothing to me. If I see you in town, I'll look through you like you don't exist. Every action has a consequence, Rab – and this one will haunt you far longer than it will haunt me.' She stepped closer. 'You don't have any power over me anymore. And if you ever come near me again… I won't be responsible for what happens next.'

Rab just stared, stunned. After everything that had happened that day, he was out of words for once. Janey almost told him she'd reported him to the police – but stopped herself. Let him get the knock on the door without warning.

Then she turned on her heel, walked out into the daylight, and didn't look back. *Damn,* she thought. *That felt good.*

Chapter 64

Scott drove Janey and Ella to their mum's house, the back of his van stacked high with Janey's bags and suitcases. He and Ella had exchanged surprised glances when Janey had lashed out at Rab, making it crystal clear she was leaving – and not coming back.

As they drove, Ella shared a bit of their family history. She told Scott how she and Janey had been in several foster homes after losing their parents in a car crash when they were young. Eventually, Nancy had adopted them, giving them the love and stability they desperately needed. Nancy wasn't just their guardian – she was their mum.

When they arrived, Scott helped Janey carry her suitcases and boxes inside, then quietly stepped back, giving the sisters space to catch up.

Just as he was about to leave, Ella ran out of the house, catching him before he could climb into his van. Without a second thought, she wrapped her arms around him in a firm hug.

'Thank you so much for everything, Scott,' she said, pulling away, her cheeks flushed with warmth. 'I'll see you at Miss Powell's later this week.'

She gave him a smile that melted his insides, and he said, 'It's no bother, Ella. Happy to help. You call me if you need anything – and I mean *anything*, Ella.' He gave one of his slow, teasing smiles, which crinkled up his blue eyes, and winked at her before jumping into the van and driving off.

Ella stood in the street, watching until the van turned the corner. She smiled to herself. *Hmmm, anything?* She pondered how good it had felt to be in Scott's arms, even for just a moment.

She skipped back into her mum's house, ready to help Janey settle in, with a warm glow in her stomach that had more to do with Scott's smile and wink than anything else.

She was delighted Janey had made the move back home, and she let herself enjoy the thought of what might happen between her and Scott. *Nothing wrong with daydreaming,* she told herself.

When Ella got home later, she told Miss Powell everything that had happened, including showing her a photo of the posters Scott had made and telling her about Rab's ban from work, which Scott had heard through the grapevine. 'Well, as far as I'm concerned, that's karma in action,' commented Miss Powell, looking thoughtful.

'What do you mean? 'asked Ella. 'Karma is based on your actions and thoughts at every moment,' explained Miss Powell. 'Rab created very negative emotions around himself and Janey. His thoughts caused him to be violent toward her. The consequences of his violent actions have now travelled beyond his control and created a scenario of *you reap what you sow.*'

'So, does that mean,' asked Ella, 'that his fate is carved out for him now? He did a terrible thing, and now many bad things will happen to him?'

'Not necessarily' continued Miss Powell. 'Karma has a strong core basis of cause and effect, and if he begins to change himself and his thoughts to more positive ones, he has the power to change his future.' She took a slow sip of tea before adding, 'Karma is simply energy. The thoughts and beliefs we hold about ourselves now will create and can affect our future.'

'So, we have the power, internally, to change our future by the way we think about things?' asked Ella.

'Exactly. He needs to change his thinking and take responsibility for his actions if he wants to create something better in his life.'

'I think I get it.' Ella looked thoughtful.

'For an example closer to home,' Miss Powell went on, 'let's look at Janey. After a few days resting here, she decided - regardless of whatever story she told us - she was going to go back to Rab - we both knew that.'

Ella's eyebrows shot up when she realised how she and Miss Powell saw right through her sister's story. 'We know she was going to return to her old life, pretend to forgive him, and then maybe in her own time find somewhere

CHAPTER 64

else to live. But you and I both could see the dangers in that. She might have forgiven him, slipped back into bad habits, and the cycle could have begun all over again.'

'So true,' said Ella. 'She could have easily fallen back into her old lifestyle without intending to, just letting life drift by.'

'Indeed. But something happened.' Miss Powell's gaze fixed on Ella. 'You took Janey somewhere... or had a conversation that changed her perspective. I'm not exactly sure what,' she admitted, her eyes searching Ella's face. 'But when you both came downstairs from the attic, she had changed her thoughts. I could hear it in her words and see it in her body language. Janey was determined not to be a victim anymore. That's karma in action, too.'

Ella knew exactly what had changed Janey's mind - her trip into the Edinburgh of old, witnessing first-hand what no choice looked like. It had been a drastic and risky move, but it had worked.

Was Miss Powell looking at her knowingly? Did she somehow realise what had happened? Sometimes, Ella felt Miss Powell knew far more than she ever let on.

Chapter 65

Ella couldn't stop thinking about the trip she'd taken with Janey through the golden mirror. The experience lingered in her mind, tugging at her thoughts over and over. She knew she had plenty to deal with in her own life, but something kept drawing her to that world beyond the mirror - a quiet pull that was getting harder to resist, tempting her to return to a time that sometimes felt more real than her own. After the past few weeks with Janey, her life felt more complicated than it should be, and part of her longed to be part of another world where she had no responsibilities.

The opportunity came sooner than she had dared hope for. The next morning, Miss Powell was meeting her friend for tea in town, so she would be out for most of the day, and Scott wasn't due around until later in the week.

She had the whole day and the house to herself, and though she knew she should probably spend it studying, today she didn't have the head for it.

What she wanted was another time-travelling adventure, something to pull her away from the ordinary and into the extraordinary again.

She made up her mind and went up to the attic, stepped behind the golden mirrored door, turned around three times, and felt the magic stir in the air around her before stepping back out into the attic again, knowing she was stepping back into another time. She shivered with excitement.

She could see through the tiny attic window that it was night time. The house and all who lived in it would be sleeping. Ella made up her mind. On this trip, she wanted her body to become solid and walk around, feeling her body instead of just being a ball of energy.

She remembered from a previous visit that by putting on clothes, her body

CHAPTER 65

would become solid and visible. This was her opportunity, as she could walk out of the house whilst everyone else slept.

Ella directed her energy to the box of chic clothes and the rail of dresses. As she slipped into a pair of wide, floaty trousers and a light camisole top, she felt a strange warmth spread across her skin. Her outline sharpened, and her legs and arms became more defined. Next, she shrugged on a green blouse, and with each button fastened, her body seemed to solidify further, becoming more real.

She rifled through the box, pulling out short stockings, and slid them over her feet. With each layer, her limbs became more visible. She slipped on a pair of shoes, tried on a jacket, and finally placed a jaunty little hat on her head.

She turned around and looked at her reflection. Staring back at her was a woman who looked more like Lily than herself, dressed in an array of beautiful, stylish clothes. She tucked her hair into her hat, squiggled up her nose and stuck out her tongue at her reflection and laughed. She surprised herself by hearing herself laugh. Now, she looked and felt like she usually did. This was going to be fun.

The house was dark and quiet, and there was no one around, just as she had suspected. She opened the back door quietly and stepped out into the garden. It was a clear night, and the garden was lit up by the full moon.

She walked up the hill, already knowing where she was going. She took a left turn at the top of the hill and headed towards the arches that would take her into the beautiful grounds of the Asylum.

As she stepped through the arches into the grounds, she was awestruck by the beauty of the night. The moon threw light all over the grounds and gardens. It shone high above the main, castle-like building that was the central part of the Asylum.

She continued to walk through the grounds, entranced by the beauty of the evening. There was no one about, and it could have almost been her own time and place. But she knew it was not. In her time, the buildings were derelict, and construction work was beginning.

She walked past the tennis courts and the beautifully maintained vegetable garden, catching the sweet smell of nightshade flowers as she walked through the garden towards the front main doors.

The entrance to the hospital was grand, featuring stone pillars and steps that led up to large wooden doors. Ella was so excited to be there in person. It was nighttime, so she expected it to be quiet and give her the chance to look around the Asylum as a real person. She knew she was taking a risk, but was sure everyone would be asleep, and she could have a look around as a real person, not just a ball of energy.

She walked up the steps in awe, pushed open the massive front doors, and climbed up more steps towards another set of heavy glass doors. She knew the great hall was just ahead to the left.

She pulled open the front door and stepped into the high-ceilinged grand hall. She took a deep breath and looked around her.

Just then, she heard the shuffling of feet and felt her arms being grabbed on either side of her body.

'Another one out for a midnight stroll, Frank,' said one of the men who had grabbed her. He had a thick Scottish accent. Ella looked at her captors by moving her head from side to side.

She had been grabbed by two big men, dressed in black trousers and shirts, wearing white aprons. She guessed they were orderlies of the Asylum.

'No, you've got it wrong, I am not a patient, I've just come out for a midnight walk because I couldn't sleep,' cried Ella.

'Likely story. No proper lady is going to be out walking in the middle of the night. Right, what's your name, and we'll put you back in the ward you belong to,' said one of the orderlies.

Ella didn't know what to say, so she said nothing. This frustrated the orderlies even more. They shoved her into a small office that was just off the main hall and locked the door behind them.

She looked around the small room. There was a fire burning in the grate, along with a small table that held a teapot, two cups, saucers, and a newspaper.

Ella looked at the date in the newspaper. It was March 9, 1939. Her stomach dropped. This was a very different time from what she usually travelled to.

CHAPTER 65

No wonder the old house had looked a little different when she had stepped back through into the attic. She hadn't given it much thought as to what period she was in. She had been too excited to go back in time again.

Ella was beginning to realise that she had no control over what date she would travel back to.

She didn't have any more time to do anything else before the two orderlies came marching back in. One of them carried a starchy-looking white coat with buckles.

They grabbed her and forced her arms in. She realised with horror that they were putting her into a straitjacket.

Damn it, she thought. *Too slow!* I should have taken my clothes off and become an invisible ball of energy again. But she hadn't moved quickly enough. Now she was trussed up like a turkey, could not move and had no means of removing her clothes.

Suddenly, the reality of the situation hit her. She was terrified. They shoved her into the corridor, and there was an ancient-looking wheelchair with restraints around the bottom wheels and arms.

They threw her into the chair and locked her ankles in leather manacles. Then, they forced a ball into her mouth and wrapped a gag around her head, so she was unable to make any noise. The ball in her mouth hurt her teeth and her tongue, and the saliva began to run down the sides of her mouth.

Then, to her ever-growing horror, the orderlies left her in the corridor like a piece of luggage.

'I'm going to finish my tea and read my paper,' said one. 'She's not going anywhere.' They chuckled and closed the door behind them.

Ella was left sitting in the corridor, unable to move or make a noise. She was barely able to breathe. She began to panic but made herself calm down and breathe slowly and deeply. She knew she needed to keep control of herself and her situation, no matter how hard this was going to be.

Ella lost track of time. She had no idea how long she had been trussed to the medieval wheelchair, in a corridor in a straitjacket with a ball and gag.

She closed her eyes and tried to meditate. She tried counting her breaths, she tried counting sheep, she tried every trick she knew to clear her mind.

She had an underlying feeling of panic deep in her stomach that was trying to creep up to her lungs, restrict her breathing and crawl up into her throat and into her brain.

Controlling that feeling of panic became her main focus.

At last, after what felt like hours, she heard the door open, and the orderlies came out. 'Damn it,' said one, 'I forgot about her. The morning shift should be changing over in an hour. Let's get her up to one of the cells, then make our rounds.'

Ella made a noise from her throat, silently begging them to take the gag off her.

'She looks familiar, this one, but I can't place her. Matron will likely know her. I wouldn't want to be in her shoes when Matron finds out that she was walking the grounds in the middle of the night,' chuckled one of the orderlies. Ella failed to see the humour in her situation.

They pushed Ella up the corridor, through many locked doors, one after another. She began to hear screams and wails of some patients as she was pushed through the corridors. This was not the type of exploration of the Asylum that she had in mind. Tears were running down her face as she realised what a terrifying situation she was in.

The orderlies pushed her through a set of double doors, and she found herself in a ward with at least twenty beds in it and a nurses' station in the middle.

The nurses were talking amongst themselves. Not quietly or respecting that it was early morning and patients were still trying to sleep. If anything, they spoke at a slightly louder level than necessary.

Ella was pushed through the ward and another set of double doors. The orderlies stopped and removed the manacles from her legs, then helped her to her feet.

She tried to shake off the stiffness from where her legs had been manacled against the chair. The two orderlies grabbed her again on either side of her body and frog-marched her up some back stairs and along another corridor. Ella had completely lost her sense of direction.

They arrived at a brightly painted yellow corridor with windows on one side

CHAPTER 65

and a series of twenty or thirty doors on the opposite side. She recognised the corridor to be very similar to the one that she had scared the horrible Dr. Ramsey in on the night of the recital. She knew what was in store for her.

They frog-marched her halfway along the corridor and threw open door number 29. They pushed her into what Ella could see was a cell.

The walls were padded, and there was only a thin mattress on the floor. High up on the outside wall was a small, barred window. There was a pot in the corner that Ella guessed was intended for use as a toilet.

They threw her in, removed the gag that was holding the horrible ball in her mouth, and she landed on the thin mattress in a heap.

She was still in a straitjacket. Her mouth was dry; the saliva had dried around her lips and dribbled down her chin. She felt useless and humiliated.

She tried to speak but found it almost impossible, as her mouth was so dry and sore from being stretched by the cruel ball and gag.

'I shouldn't be here. I am not a patient,' she managed to whisper. 'Please take me out of this jacket,' she pleaded.

The orderlies had already turned their backs on her. 'Aye, I know what you mean. She does look familiar. But if she won't give us her name, this is the best place for her for now.' He laughed cruelly. 'She'll soon find out it's best to cooperate with us. We are the ones who can make her life bearable - or hellish,' he said with a laugh. They slammed the door behind them, and Ella heard the lock click.

Could this be happening? Ella was in a padded cell, in a straitjacket, with no way of getting out, in 1939!

Suddenly, the panic that she had felt in her stomach began to rise, and the noise came out as a howl that she barely recognised as a sound coming from her own body.

It was no wonder people went mad in this place; even if they weren't disturbed when they arrived, with treatment like this, it would not take long to turn a sane person mad.

Chapter 66

In another part of the Asylum, Matron Anderson hurried along the corridor. There was much to do this morning, just as there was at the start of every shift.

One of the first things she did at the beginning of every day was check in with the night orderlies to see if they had anything to report. This morning, the orderlies reported that a patient had been walking the grounds at midnight, was uncooperative, and wouldn't give her name, so they placed her in cell 29 on the 7th floor, near Ward 18.

'She looks familiar, right enough,' said one of the orderlies, 'but we couldn't place her well enough to know her name.'

'Are you sure she is a patient? I'd best check her out first thing.' She looked sternly at the orderlies. 'What else could she be?' said the orderly, trying to justify his actions. 'Walking about at midnight - she could hardly be a respectable woman, could she?'

Matron thought about the situation. It was very unusual for a patient to be out at midnight, as all wards and rooms were locked. It would weigh on her mind until she could see for herself who this patient was and make sure she belonged here. She hurried along to cell 29.

Matron Anderson had worked in the asylum for almost twenty years. Her reputation was fierce. The wards she oversaw were renowned for being scrupulously clean and orderly. The nurses who worked under her could be sure that Matron's treatment of them and the patients would be strict but fair.

She had little time for the two orderlies on night duty. They were more

CHAPTER 66

concerned with drinking tea, playing cards, and reading the newspapers than doing a proper job. One of the orderlies was not particularly nice to the patients and had a cruel streak in him, but no patient had made a formal complaint, so nothing official could be done about the abuse they directed at patients.

Matron had already raised her concerns with the Board of Asylum Directors, but her complaint was dismissed and not properly investigated. She wondered how they had treated this so-called patient.

'We only did what we thought was right,' said the orderly with the cruel streak, whilst the other hid a chuckle under his breath.

It was their reaction that prompted Matron to hurry to the cell to see what they had done.

She had the nurse on that floor unlock room number 29. The cells were small, almost windowless, and only had mattresses on the floor.

She looked through the window first of all and saw a woman with dark hair, curled up as best she could on the thin mattress.

The matron saw, in disgust, that she was in a straitjacket. She had little respect for this method of restraint. She also saw a ball gag on the floor that must have been used as well.

She opened the door wide, stepped in, and said, 'Good morning. My name is Anderson and I am the Matron of this ward.'

Ella slowly moved, trying to shift her body and neck and stretch out her muscles, but she was so stiff it was hard to move. She wiggled up so she was almost sitting upright.

Matron gasped inwardly when she saw the young lady. She had to look twice, as she was almost the double of her favourite doctor - Dr Lily Fraser - but she knew that it could not possibly be her.

'My name is Ella, and I am not a patient here.' Her voice was barely a whisper; she was so thirsty. 'I was out for a walk enjoying the evening, and I walked into the Asylum just to have a look around and get out of the cold night air.'

Matron was horrified. Who knew who those stupid orderlies had locked away? There could be real consequences to this if this lady were telling the truth and was not a patient. Her likeness to Dr Fraser was incredible - she could almost be her sister.

'Right,' said Matron, shaking off any uncertainty. 'Nurse Peters, please remove Miss Ella's restraint jacket. I trust you are not going to give us any trouble, miss?'

'No, I promise. Besides, I can hardly move.'

The nurse approached Ella, helped her stand up, and began to undo the buckles on the back of the jacket. She helped Ella pull her arms out of it, and suddenly, Ella was free to move again.

The Matron looked at her - she was just a slip of a girl. Without hesitation, she decided to take her directly to Dr Lily Fraser and see what the best course of action was - and more importantly, find out if Dr Fraser knew this girl who looked so much like her.

Chapter 67

Dr Lily Fraser sat at her desk, surrounded by papers, filing cabinets and shelves of books. She remembered fondly her days as a volunteer here in this very hospital all those years ago.

In the 1920s, she had been told time and time again what a wonderful nurse she would make, and to put the idea of becoming a doctor behind her. A woman doctor of Psychiatry? It was a ridiculous notion, she was told.

She had become good friends with Rose, the herbal medicine lady, and watched in awe at her ability to know the right herbs to mix to help and heal people. Rose also read her tarot cards one day and showed her a future of being able to do anything she wanted when she put her mind to it. Lily didn't need the cards to tell her that – deep down, she knew that already.

She trained as a nurse and, after the first year, chose to specialise in psychiatry. She spent a year working in this field and other mental hospitals, but she knew she could do more. After a year, she enrolled in the University of Edinburgh's Medical School and persevered through the very male-dominated world of medicine. She had to study twice as hard as her colleagues, as she was constantly having to prove her capabilities.

She completed her degree with honours. In 1938, she proudly gained her position at Craighouse Mental Hospital. Since the Mental Health Act of 1930, lunatics were now called patients and Asylums Mental Hospitals.

Changes were afoot, but she knew that some brutal treatments still went on, even in her hospital.

She looked up when she heard the rap on the door. 'Come in,' she said.

Matron Anderson came into her office and closed the door behind her. Lily had great respect for the work that Matron did in the hospital.

'Dr Fraser, good morning, sorry to bother you, but I think it's important,' began Matron, 'the orderlies found a lady wandering around the building around midnight last night and decided that she was a patient even though she said she wasn't. They constrained her in what I think was an overly harsh way. The lady's name is Ella, and she insists that she is not a patient, and I can't find any record of that name. I brought her to you, as I think you will find her, well, interesting,' she said.

'Thank you, Matron, bring her in,' said Lily.

'Nurse Stewart, please bring the young woman in,' said Matron. The nurse entered the office holding onto Ella.

Ella limped in, still feeling stiff and sore. She looked up, wondering who she had been taken to and what horrible things were in store for her now. She had tried to get a moment to herself so she could slip out of the clothes and become invisible again. However, even when she asked to use the toilet, the nurse stayed with her. Disappointed and wondering what was in store for now, she reluctantly stepped into the office.

When she looked up and saw Lily in a doctor's uniform, she gasped out loud. She had not expected to meet Lily here.

As she looked at Lily, Ella could see that Lily was certainly older than when she had last seen her, but there was no doubt that it was the Lily that she knew from previous visits.

Ella tried to work out how it was that she was standing in front of her, the very woman whom she had admired 100 years ago. She remembered that just the night before, she had taken note of the date – 9th of March 1939.

Putting all the information together and knowing the date, Ella rightly assumed that Lily must have spent years studying and was now a doctor in the hospital. Ella admired her even more.

In the meantime, Dr Lily Fraser looked at Ella and found herself looking at someone with a very familiar face. Who was this girl, and why did she look so familiar to her? Was she a long-lost cousin or relative? Her bone structure, eyes and even her body shape were very similar to her own.

But ever the professional, Dr Lily did not allow this unsettling feeling to

CHAPTER 67

show to Matron. 'Thank you, Matron,' said Lily, without missing a beat, 'You did the right thing by bringing her to me. I'll take her from here.'

Matron admitted to herself that she was disappointed with the lack of reaction from Dr Lily Fraser. After all, it's not every day you come across someone who looks very much like you.

'Very well, Dr Fraser, if you need me for anything, you can call me on Ward 23 this morning,' said Matron, and bustled out of the room.

'Please take a seat,' said Dr Lily to Ella, ever the professional.

Chapter 68

Ella still couldn't believe her eyes. She had not expected to come face-to-face with Lily here in the hospital.

The doctor's voice interrupted her thoughts. 'Hello,' said the doctor, 'I am Dr Lily Fraser, head of this department. Can you tell me your name and where you are from?'

As Dr Lily looked at Ella, she couldn't help but feel that not only was her face familiar, but strangely, so were her clothes. Ella appeared to be wearing clothes very similar to those Lily herself had worn in the 1920s, the same ones she had stored in the attic of her old family home many years ago.

But how could that even be possible? Dr Lily took a deep breath as she realised the young woman in front of her was talking, and brought herself round to listen.

'I'm Ella MacDonald, and I am from Edinburgh.' Ella thought it wise not to mention her exact address, as Lily might still be living there at this time.

'Have we met?' asked Dr Fraser. 'You look very familiar.' Ella needed time to think. She asked for a glass of water to give herself a moment. The fog in her brain was beginning to clear. She stared at the stylish, strong woman in front of her and wondered why she looked so much like the old photos she had seen of her grandmother. She began to connect the train of thoughts and images that came flooding into her mind.

She thought back to the stories her father used to tell about his family. She had not thought of these stories for years. Although her mum and dad had both died when she was young, she still had some memories and had kept family photos and old letters. She vaguely remembered her father talking

CHAPTER 68

fondly about his mother, Lillian, and what a fantastic woman she was.

Ella's memories were distant and hazy. But the more she thought about it, the more she recalled her father saying what a great doctor her grandmother Lily had been. She tried desperately to remember her grandfather's name. She stared at the woman sitting in front of her - Dr Lily - the colour of her hair, the shape of her nose, her cheekbones, her mannerisms... all so familiar.

Ella closed her eyes and thought of her father. He had copper-coloured hair and distinctive cheekbones. People often told her she looked like him. She reached deeper into her memory and brought to mind a photo of her grandmother - her father's mother. She pictured the photo she had stored away in a box of letters and pictures under her bed. As the image became clear, she could not believe it.

She opened her eyes and stared at Lily. She gasped aloud and blurted, 'No... surely not. It's just not possible.' Realising what she had said, her hand flew to her mouth.

Ella came to the shocking conclusion - she was sitting in front of her father's mum! Now she knew why she had always felt connected to Lily - she was her grandmother. And she was pretty sure she shouldn't be here in front of her.

Trying to keep a clear head, she decided she must not reveal too much or change anything in history.

Dr Lily sat waiting patiently for her to speak. Despite Ella's shock, she knew she must tell Lily about her terrible experience in the hospital. She had a feeling her grandmother could do something about it - and perhaps help others in the future.

Ella took a deep breath. 'I read that you once admitted yourself as a patient to understand how the less privileged were treated. Well, last night, I experienced it for myself.'

Dr Lily's eyes widened slightly at this.

'I am not a patient, and I have no psychiatric problems. Yet, I was hauled into a locked room by two orderlies, shoved into a straitjacket, strapped into a wheelchair, and - to add insult to injury - gagged with a ball gag. I was left in a corridor like a piece of luggage.' Ella took a deep breath, determined to tell her story without tears.

'I was then taken down corridors and pushed into a padded cell. If this is how they treat someone who is well, I dread to think how they treat the ill.' She paused, looking at the woman behind the desk, confident that she was doing the right thing. 'I'm telling you this because I believe I'm only confirming what you already know - and what you need to hear from someone else.'

Just then, a tall, handsome man in a suit entered. Ella recognised him from the night of the recital. He had played the piano beautifully and stayed long after his shift to help the patients.

He nodded at Ella. 'Is everything okay here, Dr Fraser?' 'Yes, Stuart. I'm just speaking with this young lady.' He glanced at Ella again, as if he almost recognised her, then shook his head. He smiled at the doctor before leaving.

'Was that Stuart MacDonald?' asked Ella. 'Yes,' said Lily. 'Do you know him?' 'No,' replied Ella - though she knew exactly who he would become.

Stuart MacDonald was a hospital manager and union representative, and in his spare time, he advocated for patients' rights. He still loved playing the piano.

Ella was stunned. She was sure she had just met her grandfather as a young man. She had to think fast. She couldn't risk interfering with the past.

For a moment, she almost blurted out everything - the golden mirror, the future, living in Lily's house a century later. But she stopped herself. That could be a serious mistake. Dr Lily's gaze softened, but a quiet intensity lingered.

'Ella,' she said slowly, 'I can tell when someone carries a secret they're unsure how to share. I think your secret may involve perhaps a mirror... a mirror that doesn't just reflect, but transports. A mirror that knows the paths of time itself.'

She gave a faint smile. 'If that's the story you were about to tell, I don't want to hear it. Not now. But know this - you're not the first to discover the mirror's magic. You're not alone.' She let the words hang in the air.

'I'm going to leave you alone for two minutes. I'm sure you know what you need to do. And remember, Ella - you can do anything you want to do.' The

CHAPTER 68

doctor left the office, looking back at Ella one last time.

Ella didn't hesitate. She knew she was being given a way out. She stepped behind the desk and began removing her clothes. Layer by layer, she faded from view until, with her slip gone, she was once again invisible energy. She drifted through the door, past Dr Lily, who was explaining to Matron that the woman was not a patient and never would be.

Matron asked where she had gone. Lily replied, 'She's a local lass named Ella, but she's left – and if she knows what's good for her, she won't return in these times.' Matron nodded. She then told Lily she wanted to complain about the two orderlies. Lily agreed. 'I'll back you. Excessive force like that should not be used on anyone.'

They both knew change would be hard against the male-dominated board, but together, they were determined.

Ella felt Lily's warning was meant for her. She had had enough adventure for now. Floating free, she passed over the hospital gardens, watching patients tend vegetables, walk with orderlies, and enjoy the morning air. Yet she knew that behind the scenes, some still suffered.

She thought of Lily and Matron, determined to make a change from within.

Then she swept back to the corner house, through the door, and up into the attic. She stepped through the golden mirror, spun three times, and felt the shift of time and space. She emerged into the attic of her own time.

Thank goodness – she was back where she belonged.

Chapter 69

Dr Lily Fraser sat back in her chair after the encounter she had just had. She now understood exactly why Ella had looked so familiar, and it brought a flood of memories back to her.

As a young girl, she was fascinated by the golden mirror in the attic of her home. Her grandfather used to tell her stories about the magic of the golden mirror, and how it would take him to different places and times.

He was a wonderful storyteller, and Lily used to love sitting on his knee and listening to him. He was an adventurer, an explorer, a seeker of magical experiences and – according to him – a time traveller!

Lily would ask her grandfather what the secret to the golden mirror was, but he would just chuckle and say, 'If it's meant for you, lassie, you'll find out.' As a curious child, Lily had secretly gone up to the attic, found the key, turned the lock, and stepped inside the magical portal.

Nothing happened the first few times she stepped in and out of the cupboard. It made her giggle and think what a good storyteller her grandfather was. Still, she loved his tales and often visited the golden mirror.

One day, as she sat in front of it, she remembered her grandfather's stories and the message he often spoke about – the power of three.

She stepped into the space behind the golden mirror, took a deep breath, and spun around three times. Suddenly, it felt as though the walls had melted away, her body and energy swirling, leaving her dizzy and slightly sick when the spinning stopped.

When she opened her eyes, she felt her energy spill out of the cupboard and into the attic – but it looked very different. It was almost empty, clean-

CHAPTER 69

looking. The attic was the same space, yet the trunks and boxes were gone.

She felt herself floating down the stairs. The house was the same one she had always known - yet somehow, everything looked different. Gaslights flickered, casting deep shadows over the grand furniture in the hall.

Could it be true? Had her grandfather's stories been real all along? Before she could think further, a young boy came charging out of the front room.

He was a cheeky-looking lad, dressed in a fine black suit, white shirt, and bow tie. He stopped in front of Lily, screamed, spun around, and ran back into the room. 'Nanny! I just saw the ghost of a girl!' Lily heard a woman with a heavy Scottish accent reply, 'James Robert Hamilton, stop making up stories!'

'But I did see something this time!' protested the boy.

Lily realised at once - she had just met her grandfather as a little boy. She had travelled back in time. Lily had several adventures in Victorian Edinburgh before one day stepping through the golden mirror, spinning three times - and nothing happened.

She thought maybe the magic of the golden mirror had run out. Some of her adventures had been hair-raising, and she sometimes wondered if she would make it home. She hid the key away and soon it was a distant memory.

It had been so long ago that the golden mirror had started to feel more like a magical fairy tale than reality. Sometimes she wondered if it had truly happened, or if it was all in her imagination.

She thought back to when her parents had moved to the country. Lily had insisted that her friend Rose move into the house with her, her apothecary, and her young family.

Life had been busy - she was studying medicine and had met the man who would become her husband, Stuart MacDonald. She knew then her life was going to be with him and the hospital.

Before Rose moved in, Lily told her she was welcome to use the attic for storage - but not to open or use the cupboard behind the golden mirror.

When asked why, Lily had laughed and said, 'Oh, just old stories from my grandfather. I'm keeping the tradition alive.'

Her life became consumed with studying psychiatry, marrying Stuart, and securing a position – and eventually an apartment – in the very hospital where she had once volunteered.

She had almost forgotten about the golden mirror until she met young Ella that morning.

When the mysterious patient had been brought into her office, she saw a younger version of herself, dressed in old clothes from her mother's attic at her former home.

That was when all the memories of the golden mirror and her adventures came flooding back. She sensed that Ella had stepped out of her own time and into trouble.

Lily believed the best course of action was to leave Ella alone in the office – if she was who Lily thought she was, she would know what to do.

Her suspicions were confirmed when she returned and found, behind her desk, a neat pile of clothes – but no Ella.

Dr Lily Fraser did briefly wonder what time and place Ella had come from. She had no doubt they were related – it was like looking in a mirror that morning.

Because of her own experiences with the golden mirror and her grandfather's strange and wonderful tales, Lily became an extraordinary doctor of the mind.

She listened carefully to her patients' stories and visions, not assuming they were mentally ill – sometimes, she believed, great creativity was hidden within.

She saw the fine line between genius and madness, and nurtured both patients and staff to see it too.

She was among the first doctors to recognise that some minds could not thrive on mundane routines – some simply needed the freedom to create music, art, or writing.

She fought daily against the hospital board, who wished to dull people's creativity with drugs or the newly popular Electric Shock Therapy.

Dr Lily Fraser became known throughout Edinburgh's medical circles as a public voice for those living on society's edge. She helped distinguish between behaviour that was different but acceptable, and those truly suffering deep mental distress.

Over the years, with the help of her talented pianist husband, she hosted musical and performance evenings to showcase the talents of many patients – helping the public to appreciate and celebrate individual differences rather than fear them.

Chapter 70

Back in Miss Powell's familiar attic, Ella sat down on a trunk and caught her breath. She reminded herself to check the mirror to be sure she was really there.

She saw her reflection, wrinkled her nose, and smiled. Everything was going to be alright. She was back in her body, in her own time.

That had been a frightening adventure, and she was very grateful to be back. At one point, she had honestly thought she might be stuck in a straitjacket in 1939 forever.

She was still trying to wrap her head around the fact that she had been living in the very same house where her grandmother had grown up. Her trips to the past had always felt exciting, but knowing this now made them feel even more real – she had uncovered something far bigger than she ever imagined.

For most of her life, Janey had been the only family she knew. So when Ella began to piece things together, finally, the shock was tremendous. Lily – the woman she admired, who had been teaching her lessons about life, resilience, and confidence – was her grandmother. Watching and learning from Lily, and seeing how she had lived her life, was changing her, shaping the person she was becoming in the present. It was overwhelming, yet somehow it made perfect sense.

She had only a handful of memories of her parents. There had been no aunts, uncles, or grandparents in their lives, and when their parents died, it was just her and Janey, left in a world that had suddenly collapsed around them. The shock had been so immense that they barely questioned their past

CHAPTER 70

– they simply survived.

A box of family papers and photographs had been kept, their only link to the past. Now, those photographs were returning vividly to Ella's mind, fragments weaving into the present and drawing exciting connections she had never seen before.

After the shock of losing their mum and dad – and their home – they had to adjust quickly to a new life. They learnt to put up with the constant changes of new foster parents, new schools, and new friends, until they finally settled with Nancy as their latest 'mum'. As young women, they became more interested in the present moment and almost trained themselves not to think too much about the past. But now, Ella was more intrigued than ever by those who had gone before her.

She realised how naive she had been in never wondering why the golden mirror could help her time travel or who had put it there. She had no doubt now, after meeting Lily at the hospital, that her grandmother had also ventured through the mirror. Oh, how she longed to hear her stories.

Ella wondered what time it was and how long she had been away. She made her way downstairs to make herself a nice cup of tea and give herself time to think and reflect on what she had experienced.

As it turned out, it was only mid-afternoon. Ella carried a tray of tea and biscuits into the front sitting room.

The room was south-facing, so even when the sun wasn't strong, like this afternoon, the room caught the light through the four large bay windows overlooking the garden.

Miss Powell, who had been snoozing on and off, was delighted to see Ella with tea. When she had returned home that afternoon and found no sign of Ella, she had assumed she was out for the day.

'You look like you have something on your mind, lassie,' said Miss Powell. 'Do you want to share it with me?'

'Aye, I think I do, Miss Powell.'

She hesitated, wondering where to start and how much to share. 'I've been wondering lately about my family tree. Do I remind you of anyone?'

Miss Powell picked up her cup of tea, settled into her chair, and looked intently at Ella.

'Well, lassie, I have to admit, the first time you came to the house for your interview, I thought you seemed very familiar. I couldn't place your face, but I knew I felt comfortable in your company, as if I already knew you.'

Miss Powell was thoughtful. 'But I knew I couldn't truly know a young lass like you. Still, my gut told me you belonged here.'

'Please, take a good look at me now. Do I remind you of anyone you used to know?' Ella pressed.

Miss Powell studied her. 'You know, now you mention it, you do remind me a bit of my mother's friend. I knew her when I was very young.' She paused. 'In fact, this used to be her house.' Ella gasped, goosebumps prickling her arms. Now she believed more than ever that what she had learned behind the mirror was true.

The more Miss Powell thought about her mother's old friend, the more Ella's resemblance struck her. Had she subconsciously recognised it all along? Was that why she had taken Ella on without even checking her references?

Miss Powell had warm memories of her mother's friend visiting them when they lived on the other side of town. She recalled the wee flat with only a shared toilet on the landing, and her parents and herself living in one room.

Her childhood home had always been full of plants and flowers hanging to dry, jars of dried herbs and tinctures her mother prepared. Even in that tiny flat, her mother Rose would treat neighbours and friends for their ailments.

Privacy had been non-existent; their home was more like a community hub, with people coming and going at all hours.

Miss Powell smiled at the memory – the days before her family moved into this house, which had once belonged to her mother's best friend. Lily Fraser – that was her name before she married.

'How could I forget?' Exclaimed Miss Powell. 'My mother's friend was called Lily. A lovely lady she was – and my goodness, you do look like her.'

Ella was thrilled and eager to keep her talking. 'You might think I'm a bit crazy, Miss Powell, but I met Lily when she was a young woman.'

'What? I don't think so, my dear!' Miss Powell smiled, amused at such a fantastic claim. 'That's just not possible. She was twenty or thirty years older

CHAPTER 70

than me, which would put her well into her hundreds by now!'

'Well, in a strange way, I think I have. Are you ready for a great story?' Ella asked. Miss Powell nodded eagerly. She loved a good story. 'Great,' said Ella. 'But can I ask a favour? Let me tell my story without questions or interruptions, and if anything I say sparks a memory, will you share it at the end?'

'Aye, lass, I promise,' said Miss Powell, snuggling into her chair with a cup of tea, eyes sparkling. 'Well, remember that afternoon I asked you about the attic and went upstairs to potter around...'

Ella was a wonderful storyteller, describing in vivid detail her many experiences going through the golden mirror. Miss Powell's eyes misted as she listened to Ella's account of the house in the old days, of old Edinburgh, and of meeting her mother, Rose, before she was even born. She was captivated.

Ella left nothing out, and by the time she finished, day had turned to dusk. She gave Miss Powell time to process what she'd heard.

'Don't say a word for now, Miss Powell. Let it sink in, and then tell me if you still want me around as your companion after hearing my story!'

Ella didn't wait for an answer; she busied herself taking away the tea tray.

She returned, set up the coal fire, and lit it as the evening chill settled in. She turned on the lamps, bathing the room in a warm glow.

Miss Powell pondered Ella's story. The descriptions were so vivid, she knew they had to be true. She was open to believing other realms existed, and she had loved hearing about old Edinburgh and the people Ella had met. She knew them all.

Ella brought Miss Powell her supper on a tray, and they settled in front of the fire.

'I enjoyed your story, and I do believe somehow you travelled to a time gone by. I'll need time to think and gather my own memories. But don't worry - I still want you as my friend and companion! Don't you be going anywhere soon!' She chuckled.

'Can you shed any light on the people I met?' Ella asked eagerly. 'Maybe I can - but not tonight. I'm tired and would like to enjoy the story you've told me.' 'Of course,' said Ella, realising she had likely tired out her friend. 'I'll leave you to it, Miss Powell. If you don't need anything else, I'll see you in the morning.'

'I'm fine, lass. Good night – and thank you for sharing your story,' said Miss Powell.

As Ella closed the door, Miss Powell closed her eyes and drifted into her own world of memories.

Chapter 71

Meanwhile, on the other side of the city, Scott was sitting in his wee flat, happy to be home after a busy day.

Life was mostly about work at the moment, as he didn't have a girlfriend to distract him or pull him in directions he had no interest in going.

When he thought about his ex-girlfriends, that was exactly how they had made him feel - pushed and pulled into doing what they wanted, following their plans and expectations rather than his own. He didn't need or want that in his life.

Scott had a day off tomorrow and was wondering whether to head to the local pub for some company when his phone beeped with a new message. He picked it up, curious about who was thinking of him.

'If you are not busy, fancy meeting up for a drink?'

Scott checked the sender, and it made him smile to see it was from Ella. He replied straight away; he saw no point in playing games.

'Sure. Where and when?' Scott texted back.

They quickly arranged to meet at The Abbortsford Bar on Rose Street in an hour.

Scott's evening had just become far more interesting. He now had an unexpected evening with Ella to look forward to.

Was this a date - or just mates going out for a drink? Either way, he was looking forward to it, and there was none of the usual pressure he felt with other women.

This felt like going out with a mate - one he just happened to find incredibly attractive.

Chapter 72

Ella stepped into The Abbotsford Bar on Rose Street in the heart of Edinburgh. It was a traditional, warm, and cosy pub, decorated with red wallpaper with gilded borders and an island bar in the middle.

Scott was already there, sitting comfortably in the corner. The pub had red padded seats and fixed tables spaced around it, giving customers room to get to the bar and move around.

Ella felt her heart warm just by being there and her spirits lifted as she saw Scott sitting in the corner with a pint.

She squeezed in beside him, and he slid along the seat to make room for her. 'What can I get you to drink?' he asked.

'Glass of white wine, please,' replied Ella. She took off her coat and made herself comfortable. Scott smiled, got up, and went to the bar to fetch her drink.

Ella sat there, looking around the old pub and enjoying the fact that it had looked like this for over a hundred years. She felt energised, alive, and more connected with the past, present, and future than ever before.

Since her last experience behind the mirror, she felt a renewed joy in life. Lily's actions and determination inspired her, and learning she was her grandmother had filled her with absolute confidence. She could see where her strong genes had come from.

Ella had great admiration for Lily. For a woman to become a psychiatric doctor in the days when women were expected to stay at home and cook and clean was a considerable achievement.

She had learned that anything was possible, but you had to put yourself

CHAPTER 72

out there and make it happen, instead of waiting for someone else to do it for you.

She had been thinking a lot about Scott. He was a good man. He hadn't hesitated when Janey needed help, he gave Ella space when she needed it, he helped little old ladies like Miss Powell, and she trusted him.

More importantly, she fancied him. When she thought of him, her tummy tingled, and her heart began to beat faster. She could feel a rush of love endorphins explode in her head, making her feel good.

Admittedly, six months ago, she had felt the same, but she had no confidence in herself and was embarrassed to let him know, convinced he was too good-looking for her and well out of her league.

Now, after her experiences and watching Lily live her life, determined to help others and go after what she wanted, Ella knew that the only way to get what you wanted was to take chances.

She figured the worst that could happen would be him saying, 'No thanks, Ella, I'm not interested – I just like you as a friend.' She would be hurt, but she would survive, and at least she'd have tried.

Scott returned from the bar with a large glass of wine and a packet of crisps. 'More for my ale than your wine,' he chuckled. 'Are you hungry? If you are, we could grab something to eat.'

'No, I'm not hungry, thanks,' replied Ella, 'but I'm looking forward to this glass of wine, thanks.'

'Have to admit, I was glad to get your text, Ella,' said Scott. 'I was getting ready to go to my local, but more to fill the time than anything else. So, cheers!' He picked up his pint and clinked it against Ella's glass. They sat in comfortable silence for a few moments. Ella relished the warmth of Scott's thigh pressing next to hers.

She took a deep breath. 'Scott, I want you to know that I deeply appreciate having you as a friend and all you did for Janey – you know, helping her move out, and also giving that scumbag something to think about.' She looked deep into his eyes. 'Uh oh,' said Scott, 'sounds like there's a but coming – have I done something wrong?'

'No, not at all!' laughed Ella. She took another deep breath, determined to say what was in her heart. 'I don't know if you've noticed, but I like you – more than just a friend.' She turned to face him and looked straight into his blue eyes. 'I really like you, Scott.' She paused, took a deep breath and continued, 'If you'd like to, I'd love to take our friendship to the next level and see where it goes.'

At this point, Ella was tempted to go into all the reasons why he didn't have to say yes; the old Ella would have filled the silence with unnecessary explanations. But her newfound confidence allowed her to sit quietly, giving space for her words to sink in.

Scott could not believe his luck. Here was this gorgeous girl he had fancied since the day they met, making a move on him. He cupped her face in his hands and gently kissed her lips without breaking eye contact. 'I'd love to, Ella. You are beautiful, but I always thought you weren't interested – I didn't want to embarrass you or make things awkward by asking you out.'

Her eyes widened, and her pupils dilated with desire at his words. They looked at each other for a long moment, then burst into laughter, sharing a tender hug as they sat with their thighs pressed together in The Abbotsford Bar on Rose Street.

Chapter 73

Miss Powell sat quietly in her living room, the soft ticking of the clock the only sound, her thoughts lingering on the questions Ella had asked about the house and the past. They had stirred long-buried memories. Now that she thought about it, there had always been something familiar about Ella - something in her eyes, her curiosity, her love of life. Somewhere deep down, she must have recognised a distant echo of someone from long ago. Now, at last, Miss Powell understood why.

Ella had reminded her of her mother's dear friend, the lovely Lily. It had been Lily who had orchestrated her family's move into this very house, encouraging and helping them move from the cramped flat into this beautiful home more than seventy years ago.

Lily, with her calm grace and quiet authority, had been a guiding force. Miss Powell remembered how her mother, Rose, had spoken of Lily with such fondness, even as the years created distance between them. They had drifted apart a little after the move, as people often do. She had heard, through whispers and occasional letters, that Lily had become a doctor, working in the old asylum - later renamed the mental hospital. Lily had married, started a family of her own, and carved out a life for herself.

Miss Powell's mother had often recounted the story of how she had helped Lily's father overcome the shell shock that had plagued him after the Great War. With her herbs and natural healing ways, Rose had mended what the war had shattered in him. And Lily - strong, wise Lily - had never forgotten. It was that healing, that kindness, which had bound them forever, even as time pulled them in different directions.

Rose had told her daughter that Lily had felt forever indebted to her, though she had never asked for anything in return. To Rose, it had simply been the right thing to do - to help a friend, to heal where healing was needed. But Lily had understood the depth of what had been given: her father's life, restored. And when the house at the bottom of the hill threatened to stand empty when Lily moved out, it was she who insisted Rose and her family make it their own.

'You and your family should live here,' Lily had said.

Miss Powell's father had worked tirelessly to make it happen, arranging everything with the bank, and soon the small flat was just a memory. What lingered most in Miss Powell's mind from those early days of moving into the grand house was the sense of space - so much space, so much light, and such a vast garden. She had been just a child, but the move was significant.

Her mother had continued her herbal practice in the front room, the scent of drying herbs always in the air. And Miss Powell, as a young girl, had been her mother's shadow - an unofficial apprentice, soaking up the wisdom and learning the delicate balance of nature's remedies. When her mother grew older, it was only natural for Miss Powell to step into her shoes, continuing the work, becoming the healer and the reader of the house.

After her father passed, and later, her mother in the 1970s, the house became hers alone, and she took over the help and healing of friends and neighbours. Over the years, the once-bustling home eventually turned silent, but she never left. The rooms that had once held the laughter and chatter of those who came seeking cures now echoed with quiet solitude.

By the time she was in her late sixties, the world around her had changed. Health shops, new-age healing, and tarot readings had become more accepted, and the older people - those who had sought her out for decades - slowly disappeared, moving away or passing on.

Miss Powell hadn't felt the need to chase new customers. She preferred the quiet now, content to make her tinctures for herself and a few dear friends. The world outside her door grew unfamiliar - young families with children who barely noticed her or knew nothing of what she had once done moved into the houses around her. It didn't bother her. She had lived her life in the

CHAPTER 73

service of others and now found peace in the silence.

As she sat, lost in her thoughts, she heard the creak of the front door opening. Ella had returned. Miss Powell smiled softly, feeling the weight of the past lift from her shoulders. Perhaps, one day, she would tell Ella the whole story - about her mother, about Lily, and how this house had come into their lives. But not yet. There was time.

For now, Miss Powell had found the answer to a question that had been quietly lingering in her heart: Who would inherit this house, this legacy, this place of healing and love? It seemed only fitting - almost poetic - that the home should return to the hands of the granddaughter of her mother's dear friend, the woman who had gifted her family this place nearly a century ago.

The house had come full circle. And Miss Powell knew, deep down, that this was exactly how it was meant to be.

Acknowledgments

This book wouldn't exist without the love and support of so many people.

It was written during the later days of lockdown when I couldn't be in Edinburgh and was missing family and the city. Writing this was my connection to them and the city I love.

To my husband, Mario Morris, thank you for your unwavering support and endless patience throughout this journey. Your belief in me means everything.

To my niece, Joni Di Placido, and my nephew, Dani Di Placido, for reading the raw draft of the book. Your feedback and encouragement in this story from the beginning gave me the courage to keep going.

And to all my family, friends and Beta Readers who read early drafts and shared your insights – thank you for helping shape The Golden Mirror into the book it is today.

If you enjoyed this story, I'd love to hear from you!

You can connect with me at

www.veemorris.com or find me on Facebook at @veronicamorrisauthor.

About the Author

Vee Morris is a writer, performer and storyteller. She has spent years inspiring audiences with bubbles, balloons and a touch of magic at festivals and magical gatherings all around the UK and the world! Now she brings that same sense of enchantment to the page.

Her debut novel, *The Golden Mirror*, combines her love of storytelling, history, and her home city - the mystical city of Edinburgh - into a tale of courage, self-discovery, and timeless connections.

When not writing, Vee can be found exploring nature, working with tarot, co-facilitating transformational events with Magic Wizardry or creating magical items. She divides her time between Glastonbury, Wales, Scotland and the mountains of Southern Spain with her husband, Mario Morris, and their beloved dog, Buddy.

Discover more about Vee and her writing at **www.veemorris.com**

For magical happenings, live events, and transformational experiences, visit **www.magicwizardry.com**.

You can also connect with her on Facebook: **@veronicamorrisauthor**.

A Note to Readers

Thank you for reading The Golden Mirror!

If Ella's story touched you, please consider leaving a short review online.

Reviews make a huge difference in helping other readers discover the book.

Thank you!

Printed in Dunstable, United Kingdom